Helm, I thought. A mysterious character named Helm pretending to be a freelance photographer named Madden. A detective tracking down a criminal or a criminal organization? A spy or counterspy? A robber or con man setting up a big caper? In any case, it seemed that this nebulous weirdo had taken a hired plane north into the Canadian bush and wound up floating in the ocean a long way from his supposed destination minus his aircraft, his pilot, and his memory. An attractive female had then appeared, very conveniently, to claim this masquerader as her lover and intended husband, and confirm his false identity.

That was when Kitty said, "Darling, when we get to the hotel, please do exactly as I tell you. Please?"

There was something odd and strained about her voice. I glanced at her quickly. She'd taken a small, nickelplated, automatic pistol from her purse and she was pointing it straight at me.

Fawcett Gold Medal Books
by Donald Hamilton:

DEATH OF A CITIZEN

THE WRECKING CREW

THE REMOVERS

MURDERER'S ROW

THE AMBUSHERS

THE SHADOWERS

THE RAVAGERS

THE DEVASTATORS

THE BETRAYERS

THE MENACERS

THE INTERLOPERS

THE POISONERS

THE INTRIGUERS

THE INTIMIDATORS

THE TERMINATORS

THE RETALIATORS

THE TERRORIZERS

THE TERRORIZERS

Donald Hamilton

A FAWCETT GOLD MEDAL BOOK

Fawcett Publications, Inc., Greenwich, Connecticut

THE TERRORIZERS

ISBN 0-449-13865-8

Printed in the United States of America

10   9   8   7   6   5   4   3   2   1

ONE

They fished me out of Hecate Strait, off the coast of British Columbia, early on a fall morning in a heavy fog. Fortunately the ship was proceeding dead slow with a lookout at the bow who heard the plane come down. Even so, a lone man in a lifejacket is a small target at sea, and they could easily have missed me, in which case I'd have died of exposure in short order. I hadn't had far to go.

The ship was the *Island Prince*, a small, elderly freighter of Scandinavian origin which nowadays makes a weekly circuit from Vancouver, B.C., up the coast to the port of Prince Rupert, out to the Charlotte Islands, and back down to Vancouver—in case your geography is shaky, that's not too far north of Seattle, Wash. I acquired all this information afterwards, of course. At the time, I wasn't really switched on and recording, if you know what I mean. The *Prince* conveyed me to her next stop in the islands. There, a helicopter, alerted by radio, was waiting to fly me across the Strait to the Prince Rupert Regional Hospital which, serving a wide wilderness area, has a chopper pad next to the front door for just such emergencies as mine.

Well, maybe not quite like mine. Not that chartered bush planes don't crash occasionally, and I'm sure it's happened before that only the passenger survived. For the survivor to have taken a bad crack on the head during the proceedings is, I suspect, not unheard of. I have no doubt there have also been instances, maybe even in the hospital to which I'd been brought, in which the half-

5

frozen, headachy survivor couldn't at first remember a hell of a lot about what had happened to him; but in most of those cases, I'm reasonably sure, the guy soon remembered who he was. . . .

"Paul, darling!" That was Kitty, bursting into my hospital room without knocking, as usual, carrying a newspaper and an armful of flowers. Well, she said she was Kitty. You couldn't prove it by me. Actually, her real name was Catherine Davidson, or so she'd told me after learning of my memory problem. She'd said I might as well use the nickname since I always had. Now she dropped the paper on the bed, got a fresh grip on the flowers, and looked around the room in a baffled way. "Where the devil should I put this stuff?"

She had the special, intriguing Canuck accent that manages to sound British without putting you in mind of either an 'arf-and-'arf London Cockney or an I-say-old-chap Limey aristocrat, but I wouldn't have wanted to try to explain how I acquired the background for this linguistic comparison. In some respects, the mental computer seemed to be quite cooperative. It simply balked at handing out data on one subject. Me.

"You might try the bedpan," I said.

"Gratitude!" she said. "That's what a girl gets for trying to brighten the patient's day."

I eyed the enormous bouquet warily. "How do you know I don't have hay fever?"

"Well, if you do you never told me about it. Do you?"

"Are you kidding?" I asked. "If I don't know who I be, ma'am, how can I know what chronic diseases I is or ain't got?"

There was a little silence. Kitty got rid of her burden by cramming it into the water pitcher on the dresser. She slipped off the long, dramatic coat she was wearing and dropped it on a chair. She came back to the bed.

"I'm sorry, dear," she said. "I keep forgetting. . . . It's no better?"

"No, ma'am. All I know, besides what you tell me, is what I read in those Vancouver papers you bring me; and I still can't make heads or tails of your lousy Canadian politics. What the hell is a Socred?"

"Social Credit. One of our political parties." She spoke absently, looking down at me; then she smiled. "Well, it doesn't matter all that much, does it? I mean, what you don't remember. It will come back to you. In the meantime I know perfectly well who you are. You're Paul Horace Madden, of Seattle, a very good free-lance photographer, and a very nice person I'm going to marry as soon as he gets on his feet again, and he'd better not be too slow about it, or I'll just crawl right into that hospital bed with him."

Looking at her, I wondered if that part of the world was full of beautiful women in baggy pants, or if she was a unique specimen. Instinct told me that, while her unbecoming taste in clothes might be currently commonplace in the great Northwest, and even elsewhere, this girl wouldn't ever be commonplace anywhere. She was a tallish, very slender, brownhaired kid with a small, lovely, pink-cheeked face. There's something about a damp, cool, coastal climate that seems to produce that kind of fresh-faced loveliness; but again, don't ask me how I knew it. I couldn't really remember any other damp coastal climates or any other fresh-faced lovelies. The thought just came to me.

She was wearing a pink pullover sweater over a pink open-necked shirt; and pink slacks that were, as I've indicated, ridiculously wide, so they had a sloppy-floppy look in spite of being immaculate and sharply creased. It was a garment that obviously hadn't been picked for flattery, or even practicality, just for current style. Nevertheless, she surmounted the handicap with ease, and managed to leave me with no doubt that her unseen legs were shapely and marvelous, and her invisible ankles slim and wonderful. The idea of sharing a bed with her, by invitation, wasn't exactly revolting. From what she'd already said to me, and to the authorities who'd questioned me about the crash, this wouldn't be the first time it had happened. It seemed ungallant of me to have forgotten it.

I said firmly, however, "Begging your pardon, ma'am, what I want right now is to get me out of this damned bed, not you in. First things first and all that. Not that

7

I don't appreciate the offer. I'll be happy to accept a rain-check valid for a more suitable time and place."

She made a face at me and laughed. "Well, all right, I won't rape you today if you're feeling shy, darling. . . . What do the doctors say? Have they told you when you'll be well enough to leave?"

I said, "I have a hunch they'd turn me loose right now if I wasn't such a fascinating specimen. They're waiting around expectantly, hoping to be present when it all comes back to me in a great flood of beautiful memories." I grimaced. "Let's go through it again, Kitty. If you don't mind."

She winced. "Oh, dear, we've been over and over. . . . But of course I don't mind if you think it may help." She sat down on the edge of the bed. "Where do you want to start?"

I noticed that the street-sweeping pink slacks weren't quite immaculate after all. She'd got the cuffs a bit damp, getting here from the motel where she was staying in town. I glanced at the window and saw that outside it was raining vigorously. This came as no great surprise, since it had hardly stopped since I'd been well enough to notice the weather. It was a wet damned corner of the world.

I said, "Let's start with the fact that I'm P. H. Madden and live in Seattle. 2707 Brightwood Way, Bellevue, you told me. What's a Bellevue?"

"It's a Seattle suburb. Hilly. Your house is on a fairly steep little street. The lot slants right up from the side-walk; you have to climb a lot of steps to get to your front door, which is actually at the side of the house." Kitty's voice sounded mechanical, as well it might. As she'd said, we'd been over and over it. She went on: "Or you can drive into the garage at street level and let yourself into the basement, where you have quite an elaborate dark-room, all spotless and shiny like a laboratory. Then you go up a flight of stairs to the living area. Not so tidy, that, if you don't mind my saying so. Kitchen. Living-dining room. Two bedrooms and bath. You use one of the bedrooms for an office. Lots and lots of filing cabinets full of pictures. There's a porch or sundeck

8

at the front of the house, over the garage." She regarded me hopefully. "Does that bring anything back?"

It was detailed and convincing, but I didn't recognize it as a house in which I'd ever lived. "Not a thing. I gather I haven't been in residence too long. Six months or so, you said."

Kitty nodded. "Yes, you'd spent a good many years moving around, you told me. Free-lance photography in odd corners of the earth. More recently you took pictures for some magazine in Vietnam and got yourself badly wounded. Afterwards you did some work for an oil company in the Middle East, I think, and also up in Alaska—something to do with the pipeline. But you finally got tired of the nomadic life and decided to find a place where you could set up a permanent head-quarters and take the kind of pictures you really liked."

I thought about it for a little, and shook my head. "Still no contact, I'm afraid. You'd think a man would remember getting shot up in Vietnam, wouldn't you?" It was funny that I'd know about Vietnam in a general way without being able to remember a thing about me in Vietnam, but I was getting used to such mental quirks. I shrugged. "Okay, let's try something else. I take pictures for a living. Outdoors stuff, you said."

"Well, mostly. You're especially good with animals and birds; you're very good in the woods and very patient. We once had a fight, sort of, when you took me along and I kept fidgeting, you said. I thought I was sitting still as a rock. You have all kinds of elaborate equipment for taking pictures by remote control, or from a long ways off. Of course, you do other things besides wildlife. Fishing and hunting stories, articles on oil and mining and logging. . . . I told you, that's how we met."

"Tell me again."

"Well, all right, although it seems a little. . . ." She checked herself, and drew a long breath, and recited: "I work for the Malaspina Lumber Company, in their Vancouver office. I'm a public relations girl, I guess you'd say. You were doing an article on the lumber industry and I was assigned to help you. For instance, I arranged for a company helicopter to take you where you wanted

9

to go back in the bush. Things like that."

"But it wasn't a helicopter I used this last time out."

"Oh, no," she said. "That was a float plane, a De-Haviland Beaver, I believe, that you'd hired down by the waterfront. It's a safe guess; everybody flies them. The outfit is called North-Air. The pilot's name was Walters, Herbert Walters. You'd flown with him before. I was in the East, visiting our Toronto office. I didn't even know you'd been through Vancouver until I got back and found a message saying that you'd called and would call again on your way south. . . . Only you didn't. The next thing I knew, you'd been picked up way up there by Queen Charlotte Islands."

"And you don't have any idea what I was working on?"

She shook her head. "Nobody does, darling. You didn't mention it to anybody at North-Air, apparently, unless you told Walters after you were airborne. All they know is that you wanted to be taken to a small lake you'd visited before, pretty well inland. They have no idea how you came to be floating around in the ocean over a hundred miles to the north and west."

I grimaced. "I'm afraid the investigators from that Ministry, whatever it was—"

"The Ministry of Transport, or MOT as we call it. They look into all aircraft accidents."

"Sure. The Ministry of Transport. Well, somehow I got the impression they weren't exactly happy with me; and neither was that plainclothes guy from your Royal Canadian Mounted Police, the darkfaced character who stood back while they questioned me and tried to look like part of the furniture. I'm still trying to figure out what the hell they suspected me of. Am I supposed to have murdered the pilot, wrecked the plane, hit myself over the head, and taken a swim in the fog, all just for fun?"

Kitty laughed. "Oh, I don't think they have any immediate plans for throwing you into prison. It's just that, well, amnesia is a rather odd—" She stopped, abashed.

"Yeah, odd," I said.

"I'm sorry, I didn't mean. . . . Anyway, we don't seem

to be gaining on it, as you Yankees say."

I patted her on the knee. "Don't give up yet. Let's hear about the interesting stuff, like how I managed to acquire a Canadian fiancee, living way down there in the U.S. of A."

She smiled. "After our business dealings, you seemed to find your way across the border fairly frequently, Mr. Madden. Of course, you'd been doing quite a bit of work up here already, before we met, and it's only a hundred and twenty miles, freeway all the way."

"Still, it's a drive," I said. "I must have been hard up for girls."

She glanced at me quickly, then she laughed. Her laughter stopped. We regarded each other for a moment. She leaned over to be kissed. It turned out to be a fairly complicated osculation, since we'd started from positions not ideal for the purpose. Sitting in the bed, I had to kind of haul her into place across my lap, and make a number of preliminary adjustments, before we could make satisfactory contact. Once I found them, her lips were soft and eager. The chaste resolutions I'd announced earlier didn't last very long; but those damned pink slacks proved to be seriously obstructive. For the moment, at least, I had to confine myself to investigating the warm girl contours through the thin gabardiny cloth. . . .

"Paul, no!"

I sighed, surrendered the zipper tab I'd discovered, and let her go. Anyway, it was nice to know that, memory or no, the proper stimuli still produced the proper reactions, if you want to call them proper. Kitty sat up and pushed the long, straight, brown hair back from her small face. Her cheeks were flushed and she looked very pretty indeed—well, if you like phonies.

"Sorry, ma'am," I said stiffly. "I thought I heard somebody talking big stuff about getting into beds and raping people and stuff, but I must have been mistaken. My most humble apologies, ma'am. I surely didn't mean to get familiar, ma'am."

She said irritably, not looking at me, "Oh, don't be stupid! I just. . . . You're not all *that* well yet; and any-

11

way, the door isn't locked and the nurse is apt to stick her head in any minute."

"Oh, dearie me," I said sourly, "does anybody get to be a nurse without discovering that people kiss people?"

"Well, I just don't like to get all mussed and excited when . . . when it isn't really *practical*, darling."

"Sure."

She rose and looked down at herself and made a face at her slightly disintegrated appearance. She tugged the dislodged zipper back into place, pulled up her pants, tucked her shirt in, and smoothed down her sweater.

"I . . . I'll come back again tomorrow," she said, and fled, snatching up her coat on the way out.

Frowning, I watched the door close automatically behind her. I was feeling rather frustrated, but also a bit ashamed of myself for deliberately pushing her clear to the point of protest. A gentleman would have controlled his base impulses as soon as he sensed that the lady disapproved; but I wasn't a gentleman, I was a guy with a bandaged head and no memory trying to find out a few things about myself and other people. Now I was feeling puzzled and baffled and disturbed by what I'd learned.

My pretty fiancee had led everybody to believe that we'd anticipated our forthcoming marriage on numerous occasions. She'd been quite brazen about it—or modern, if you prefer. Yet the simple fact seemed to be that we didn't even know each other well enough to kiss each other without a lot of preliminary fumbling. My memory might be faulty, but I had a distinct impression that people who'd been lovers for months, as we were supposed to have been, could generally manage to find their way into a clinch more expertly than that.

The telephone rang. It startled me; then I decided it had to be Kitty calling to straighten things out between us. I sighed and picked up the instrument.

A man's voice spoke in my ear: "Helm?"

The voice meant nothing to me, and neither did the name. "What's a Helm?" I asked.

"You are," said the voice, and the phone went dead.

TWO

I replaced the instrument slowly. Then I sat there for a while, trying to put my small, safe, comfortable world back together. It had been a peaceful hospital existence with nothing to worry about except getting well. Okay, so I had a spot of amnesia; I could live with it. Sooner or later the past would return. Even if it didn't, well, nobody dies from loss of memory. What I'd misplaced probably wasn't priceless judging by what had emerged to date: some free-lance photography in the far-off boonies, a bit of non-combatant war experience—well, maybe my history was a little more colorful than some, but it still wasn't anything I couldn't afford to forget.

What had mattered was that I was alive, I was being well looked after, I had a lovely fiancee willing to share my problems, and I had a home and business waiting for me down in the U.S. Some officials had asked me some searching questions, to be sure, but that had been just part of the normal post-airplane-crash routine. I was a fairly ordinary guy named Madden who'd had a narrow escape from death and whose job was simply to regain his strength and pick up his life where he'd left it.

That was the way it had been. Now it was gone, wiped out by a kiss and a phone call. My lovely fiancee was a sweet little fraud. My name wasn't Madden. . . .

I drew a long breath and told myself to relax. Maybe I was taking the whole thing too seriously. I was, after all, not exactly a picture of perfect health at the moment —either physical or mental health. I could be building a couple of minor incidents into a major crisis simply because my recent harrowing experiences had left me vulnerable. Maybe Kitty Davidson was, as she'd claimed, just a fastidious young lady who couldn't bring herself to risk the embarrassment of being caught wrestling happily and sexily with a man, even a man she was going to marry, on a rumpled hospital bed behind an unlocked door. Maybe. And maybe the phone call had been a hoax or a joke perpetrated by a crank or a prankster—but up here in remote Prince Rupert, B.C., who'd bother?

Instinct warned me that it was serious and that I'd damned well better take it seriously. I might be reading too much into Kitty's reaction, but nobody would call up a hospital patient with a grave psychological problem and toss a strange name at him just for fun. Helm. It still didn't mean anything to me. The steering control of a boat. An old-time military skull-protection device. A patronym of Nordic or German origin.

Helm. If I was Helm, as the voice had indicated, who was Madden, if there was a Madden?

But there had to be a Madden. With the probable death of the pilot to investigate, with the sole survivor of the crash claiming ignorance on the grounds of amnesia—amnesia, for God's sake, the refuge of every impulse murderer whose mind suddenly went blank, your Honor, totally blank—the Canadian authorities would inevitably have checked me out at least as far back as the house at 2707 Brightwood Way, Bellevue, Washington. I'd be very much surprised if they hadn't checked a lot farther. There simply had to be a Madden living at that address who took pictures for a living and had a convincing background, or the questioning to which I'd been subjected would have been a lot longer and tougher.

I remembered the blocky, dark gent in plainclothes from the Royal Canadian Mounted Police. He'd been doing a lot of heavy thinking behind his deadpan expression. Even with Kitty making a positive identification, he would have found any obvious discrepancies in my record if there had been some to find. So Madden must exist—or must he? After all, I'd been told that he'd only made his appearance in the Seattle area some six months ago.

Was there, perhaps, just a guy named Helm who'd rented a house, set up a darkroom, and handed out business cards with a name that wasn't his? If so, why? And if so, why was Miss Catherine Davidson supporting the masquerade with outrageous hints about our beautiful sex life together, when she was actually, it seemed, a fairly inhibited kid who recoiled in near panic from a man's hand on her fanny, not to mention on the zipper tab of her stylish slacks?

Helm, I thought. A mysterious character named Helm, pretending to be a free-lance photographer named Madden. A detective tracking down a criminal or a criminal organization? A spy or counterspy? A robber or con man setting up a big caper? In any case, it seemed that this nebulous weirdo had taken a hired plane north into the Canadian bush and wound up floating in the ocean a long way from his supposed destination minus his aircraft, his pilot, and his memory. An attractive female had then appeared, very conveniently, to claim this masquerader as her lover and intended husband, and confirm his false identity. . . . Nuts! It was TV stuff, I told myself irritably. I was building a melodramatic soap opera out of a word spoken on the phone and the fact that a nice girl had behaved in a sensible and ladylike manner instead of succumbing wantonly to my crude advances.

My head had begun to ache. I reached for the newspaper on the bed and forced myself to shove the wild speculations out of my mind. The attending psychiatrist had said I shouldn't allow myself to get disturbed or excited, ha! I told myself that the news, as funneled through the Vancouver press, deserved my most careful attention. Reading resolutely, I learned that people were passing, or hoping to pass, or hoping to keep from passing, laws against cigarettes, dogs, guns, old age, and automobile accidents, to mention only a few of the subjects being considered for legislative remedies. The French-speaking citizens of Canada were demanding their linguistic rights, whatever those might be. The commercial fishermen were demanding protection against the depredations of foreign fishermen. The Canadian political parties were still calling each other names. So much for the overall picture.

On the local level, the recent heavy rains—I was glad to see somebody around the place admitting it had actually been raining kind of hard—had flooded certain roads in the Vancouver area and washed out most of a small town over on Vancouver Island. Don't get confused: that Captain Vancouver covered a lot of territory. The city of Vancouver is one thing: a metropolis of close to half a million inhabitants situated on the mainland. Vancouver Island is something else again: a rugged, offshore piece of real estate almost three hundred miles long. The capital of the province, Victoria, is out on this island. The two cities are connected by a system of ferries, one of which had just been bombed, providing the big news of the day:

FERRY EXPLOSION KILLS THREE
Reformo Leader Among Victims of Terrorist Bomb

Grateful for something interesting enough to take my mind off my own troubles, I read the story carefully. Apparently, the explosives had been left in an old Ford van on the car deck, and timed to go off just as the ferry, having made its fifty-mile crossing of the Strait of Georgia, was docking at Tsawwassen—don't ask me how to pronounce it—at the mainland end of the run. Fortunately, in loading, the van had got parked at the end of the vessel instead of in the more crowded and vulnerable middle. Fortunately, also, there had been some fog to delay the crossing; the explosion had therefore occurred while most passengers were still on the upper decks, instead of as they were returning to their cars, near the bomb, in preparation for landing. Even so, a dozen people had been injured and three of these had died, including a well-known Canadian politician of whom I'd never heard, who'd stayed in his car to work on a campaign speech to be delivered in Vancouver. His name had been Andrew McNair, and he'd been the head of the Reform Movement, whatever that might be, known in Canadian political shorthand as Reformo.

16

Quick work by the ferry's crew had contained the fires that had been started on the car deck. The captain had managed to dock the damaged vessel and disembark the passengers in orderly fashion. However, the continuing threat of fire, and the possibility of exploding gas tanks, had made it imperative to get everyone ashore immediately, without waiting for the police. In the confusion some people had got away from the landing area before it could be blocked off—among them, apparently, whoever had driven the van aboard, presumably in a car driven by confederates.

There was a description of the damage, as far as it had been determined at press time. The idea that the bomb could have been planted by enemies of McNair, apparently a somewhat controversial figure, was rejected on the grounds that the police had discovered in one of the restrooms, aerosol-sprayed on the wall of a booth, a known terrorist symbol, the letters PPP. The newspaper didn't mention whether the plumbing facilities involved were designed for masculine or feminine patronage. It did state, however, that the same initials had been found in a restroom after the San Francisco bus station blast last year, that had taken seven lives. What they stood for was still not known, or if it was, nobody was saying. The reporter finished his piece with a summary of all recent bombings of presumably terrorist origin: the La Guardia airport explosion, the Toronto railroad bang, and several others. He didn't say that the unknown PPP organization was responsible for all of them, but he didn't say it wasn't. . . .

Somebody knocked on the door of my room. Nurses and other hospital functionaries either don't knock at all or knock and walk right in. I waited, but nobody appeared. The knock came again. I drew a long breath. It was probably either the Mounties or the Ministry of Transport. I wondered a bit uneasily what the hell they wanted now.

"Come in," I called, and the door opened.

The girl who entered looked much too small to be a Mountie, and she didn't resemble any investigator I'd encountered to date. I told myself I'd never seen her before in my life.

"Hello, Paul," she said.

Obviously I'd told myself wrong.

THREE

She came forward rather hesitantly. She was small and slender, with heavy black hair cut short about her face, which was delicately pretty in an Oriental way. You had to hand it to Mr. Madden I reflected. Whether or not he really existed, he certainly knew how to pick them, even if his tastes did run to girls so slim they hardly cast shadows. Or maybe the choices had been Helm's, whoever he might be.

The girl was wearing a very neat, very tailored, very occidental tweed suit with a skirt, not pants. The rare, precious sight of a pair of nice girl-legs in nylons was almost too much for me to bear in my weakened condition. She wore little plastic boots to protect her high-heeled shoes from the rain, and carried a big purse and a red raincoat.

It was time for me to say something. "Hi," I said.

She stopped by the bed and looked at the paper I still held. "Isn't it terrible?" she said. "That ferry, I mean. I read about it on the plane coming up from Vancouver; one of the boys had a delivery to make near here."

"Terrible," I agreed.

My visitor looked down at me for a moment. "I don't mean to intrude, Paul," she said. "You once made your feelings about clinging females quite clear, and I'm most certainly not trying to. . . . Well, never mind that. But I just couldn't bear to think you might be lying up here wondering if I . . . if we . . . if anybody at North-Air was blaming you for what happened to Herb." She stopped. I didn't say anything. She went on quickly, speaking with just the slightest hint of a Chinese accent, "We don't, of course. To blame you for hiring him to fly would be ridiculous; flying was his business. In fact, it was very nice, very fair of you to continue to come to us when you needed a plane in spite of . . . in spite of everything. It certainly wasn't your fault that it turned out this way. After all, you don't know anything about flying; and whatever happened I'm sure you couldn't possibly have prevented. . . . They say you don't really remember what happened. That's often the case in a bad crash, I understand. I just didn't like to think you might be, well, delaying your recovery by brooding about it. Even if we're no longer . . . even if we're not on very good terms, Paul, the least I can do is to be fair, too."

"Sure," I said. "Fair."

She studied me for a moment longer. "Well, that's all I came to say, I'd better get back to the plane before they fly off and leave me," she went on. "I . . . I miss Herb very much, of course, but I'm glad you came out of it all right, I really am. I hope you get well soon." She started to turn away.

"Wait," I said.

She paused and glanced back over her shoulder in a reluctant way. "Please. Everything we had to say to each other, we said several months ago. I was just doing my duty as a Girl Scout. Don't make me regret—"

"What's your name?" I asked.

She stood perfectly still for a long time. In the silence, I could hear the inevitable rain beating against the window, and the sound of somebody rolling some kind of a cart down the hosptial corridor outside. Slowly, she turned to face me again.

"Are you serious?" she asked.

I said, "They told me that I'm Paul Madden, and that I'm engaged to be married to a wonderful girl named Catherine Davidson. They didn't tell me anything about you."

She said without expression, "That's hardly surprising, if your fiancee was doing the telling." When I didn't speak, the Chinese girl went on, "I heard from the MOT inspectors that you couldn't remember much about the crash, but they didn't say. . . . I didn't dream. . . ."

When she stopped without finishing the sentence, I said deliberately, "As you'll notice, I remember my English real good. I even recall some Spanish words, and there are a couple of other languages with which I seem to be slightly acquainted. I remember what happens when you add, or multiply, two and two. I can tell you about the American Revolution and the Civil War—otherwise known as the War Between the States—and a couple of World Wars and some unpleasantness in Korea. I even seem to know, in a general way, that there was a more recent conflict in Vietnam, but although I'm supposed to have attended the party with a camera, I remember nothing about that. I can tell you a bit about what New York looks like, or Seattle, or Vancouver, B.C., but I just don't see myself in those pictures either, if you know what I mean. I don't know when I was there if I was there, or what I did there, or whom I met there. Okay?"

She said softly, "You might have stopped me before I made a goddamned little fool of myself!"

It seemed, somehow, like a shocking thing for a Chinese girl to say, but I couldn't have told you exactly why.

"I had to let you talk," I said. "I'm sorry, but you might have said something that would trigger total recall."

"Did I?"

I shook my head. "No recall at all. Back to Square One." After a moment, I went on slowly: "I can use all the information I can get. It doesn't have to make me out a nice guy."

She frowned, staring at me hard, trying to decide whether or not I was kidding her. Well, that was something I was getting hardened to. Amnesia seemed to bring out the cynic in a lot of people.

"All right," she breathed at last. "Maybe it's a game, but all right, Paul, I'll play it with you." She paused to organize things in her mind, and began to speak in clipped, businesslike sentences. "My name is Sally Wong. I work for North-Air. I'm the girl behind the counter in the ticket office. We met about six months ago, right after you'd moved to Seattle, I believe. You'd driven up here to take some pictures at a local bird sanctuary. Afterwards you hired a plane from us to take you to a lake up north where you camped for several days photographing some rare ducks or something. We picked you up on schedule. You seemed to like your pilot, Herb Walters. After that, you did all your flying with us. At the time, Herb and I . . . well, he was in love with me and I couldn't make up my mind. Then you and I began to. . . ." She stopped, and made a small, helpless gesture. "You can fill in the blanks for yourself, can't you? It was . . . very nice for a while. Finally you met another girl on a job you were doing for a magazine. Maybe I'd started taking things a bit too seriously for you. Anyway, it was not a very good scene as the kids say nowadays. Luckily for me, there was big, strong, loyal Herb waiting patiently for me to come to my silly senses. . . ." She shrugged her small shoulders inside the neat tweed jacket. "That's it, Mr. Amnesia. I hope it helps. We Wongs are known for our fine humanitarian impulses."

She turned sharply and hurried to the door.

"Miss Wong." Since I didn't remember her at all, I didn't feel entitled to call her Sally, no matter how well we'd known each other once.

"Yes?" she said, pausing with her hand on the knob.

"Thanks."

She threw a quick look my way. I was disturbed to see that her eyes were wet. She opened the door and was gone. After a while I got out of bed. My legs were still moderately feeble, but they didn't collapse under my weight; after all, I'd been making the brave journey to the john for several days. I stood in front of the dresser and took stock, seeing a tall, skinny character in wrinkled pajamas with a neat white bandage on his head. The guy, Madden or Helm or whoever the hell he might be, didn't look like much of a lady-killer, but I guess you never can tell.

That night I dreamed about my boyhood. Awakening in the dark, with the hospital silent around me, I realized it hadn't been a dream at all. At least I didn't think it had, although the images started receding and disintegrating when I tried to call them back and study them for details. Still trying, I went back to sleep.

Before visiting hours the following morning we went through the usual hospital routine. The physical doctor, an older man named DeLong, took off the head bandage and replaced it with a slightly oversized bandaid. He told me all vital signs were positive and as far as he was concerned I was just loafing around taking up valuable space needed by sick people. Then the mental doctor had his turn. He was a young, intense, somber specimen with a big aquiline nose in a thin, dark face; the introspective kind of mind specialist who'd probably got interested in the way other people's minds worked while worrying about the workings of his own. His name was Dr. Lilienthal. We hadn't got chummy enough to proceed beyond that.

I told him I was feeling better, which was true. I told him I'd had a midnight dream about the past. I refrained from mentioning the mysterious telephone call. After all, he was a doctor, not a detective.

"Yes, I do think we're making progress," he said when I'd finished. "However, you've been through a rotten experience and your mind is apparently still trying to protect you from it. Like many self-appointed protectors, the mind sometimes over-reacts." He hesitated. "If you feel up to it, Mr. Madden, I'd like for us to do a bit of probing. We've been more or less letting things progress at their own pace while you regained your strength, but now that Dr. DeLong has pronounced you reasonably fit, let's see if we can't expedite matters a bit. Tell me about this boyhood incident you recalled in your dreams. What was it concerned with?"

"Hunting," I said. "Dove hunting. With my father."

He looked a little shocked. "*Dove* hunting?"

I grinned. "Cut it out, Doc. Don't give this ex-farm-boy that tired old bird-of-peace routine." Things did seem to be coming back; up to that moment I hadn't been aware I'd ever lived on a farm—actually, I had a vague feeling we'd called it a ranch. I went on: "That's the greatest little game bird on this continent, and where's your bedside manner? If I'd said I was a homosexual psychopath with sado-machochistic tendencies, you'd

23

merely have nodded wisely; but when I mention shooting perfectly legal game in season you act like I'd cut my mother's throat with a dull knife."

He considered resenting it; then he laughed instead. "Touché, Mr. Madden. Perhaps I'm just a naive city boy at heart. Go on, tell me about your dove hunting."

"In my dream, if that's what it was, we had a dog with us," I said slowly. I closed my eyes and I saw it clearly once again, and felt the sunshine and tasted the desert dust. "A big German Shorthaired Pointer named Buck. That was back when the GSP wasn't as popular in the U.S. as it is now. Old Buck had been imported straight from Europe by a wealthy rancher, a friend of Dad's, who'd then had a heart attack. He'd given Buck to Dad so a good dog wouldn't be, well, wasted on somebody who couldn't hunt him right." I opened my eyes. "Sorry, I'm rambling."

"That's fine. Just keep on rambling."

I said, "You don't use a pointing dog to find doves, of course, not like when you're hunting pheasants or quail. . . . You're sure you want all this? I seem to have to work around it a bit before I can get a grip on it."

"Go on."

"With doves," I said, "you just scout around until you find a place they're using, a field or spring or gravel pit, and you hide in the bushes and take them as they fly by. We worked Buck as a retriever on doves, to locate and bring in the birds that fell. They're hard little devils to find in any kind of cover without a dog, and Dad was very particular about shooting game and letting it go to waste. That evening, I remember, we were late getting home because we'd spent half an hour stomping through some tall weeds locating my last bird. Buck had been retrieving for Dad and hadn't seen it drop, but he finally found it. If we hadn't, we'd still be out there looking for that dove, I guess. Dad wasn't about to have a good day ruined by a lost bird."

I stopped. I could now see us clearly, getting out of the old pickup in front of the house, letting Buck jump out of the rear on command, and gathering up the guns and hunting vests and shooting stools. It was a long reach for me into the pickup since I hadn't got my height yet. Dad had gone ahead to open the gate. He was waiting while I got a good grip on all my gear so I could follow.

He was speaking: "That was a fine shoot, Matthew, but we must rest that field tomorrow or we will burn it out; the doves will become frightened and stop using it." He didn't have a Scandinavian accent as much as a Scandinavian way of speaking. He went on: "Now you go feed the dog while I start plucking the birds. . . ."

I had a sharp picture in my mind of him standing there in his beatup Stetson and worn ranch clothes with the old Model 12 Winchester that had a slip-on rubber recoil pad to lengthen the stock to fit him, since he was a tall, long-armed man. He'd never, that I remembered, got around to having a longer stock made although he was always talking about it. I could see the little swinging gate and the rural-type mailbox on a post. The lettering on the box was easy to read: *Rt. 4, Box 75, Karl M. Helm.*

Helm. Matthew Helm, son of Karl and Erika Helm. Just as the man on the phone had said. It was confirmed now; I could go on from there. I was Matthew Helm, profession unknown, alias Paul H. Madden, free-lance photographer; but why the masquerade? The answer to that question, along with the more recent part of my life to which it belonged, remained unremembered, but other things were coming back. . . .

FOUR

Somebody was talking to me. I came back across the years from the dry, sunny, southwestern country of my boyhood to the sterile northwestern hospital room with rain on the window.

"What did you say, Doctor?" I asked.

"Are you all right, Mr. Madden?"

"I'm fine," I said.

It was a time to be very careful. I now knew for certain that I was a man who'd constructed a false identity for himself and worn it for at least six months—and had then, somehow, wound up in the ocean with a cracked head. The two circumstances might have no connection, but I couldn't count on that. It was no time to be passing out personal information to anybody, beyond what was absolutely necessary to keep them happy and unsuspicious.

"I guess I was thirteen or fourteen at the time," I said. "Later, I recall getting kicked out of college due to some kind of fight I got into with a bunch of upper-classmen who were trying to push me around." I grinned. "I must have been a feisty young fellow. I finished up at another school. Then my parents both died within the same year. I got a job with a camera on a newspaper in the state capital, Santa Fe, New Mexico. Later I worked for some other New Mexico newspapers. I did say all this took place in New Mexico, didn't I? After that—"

I stopped abruptly. It had been coming with a rush, but suddenly there wasn't any more.

"Go on."

"That's it," I said. "That's all she wrote, at least for now. It ends with that last newspaper job—the last I remember, anyway. That was in Albuquerque. I don't remember leaving, and there's nothing after that."

"I see," he said. He frowned thoughtfully, watching me, for a second or two. Abruptly, he got up and walked to the window and spoke looking out at the rainy view. "Mr. Madden."

"Yes."

"I'm inclined to turn you loose. Physically, Dr. DeLong tells me you're coming along very well. Mentally, I feel you can't be helped much more here. There's no skull fracture. The concussion seems to have produced no impairment of function. The danger of hematoma—blood clots—is past. As far as your memory is concerned, I think you can deal with the problem yourself. If it comes back, fine. If not, as I told you earlier, it's something most patients adjust to quite easily, although their friends and families tend to take it more seriously." After a little pause, he swung around at the window to face me once more. "However, if you think you're up to handling it, I'd prefer to send you off with all the information we can give you."

"What information?" I asked. "Don't tease me, Doctor."

He said carefully, "We're in possession of some rather puzzling data—rather disturbing, I might add."

I realized, from the way he was studying me, that for all his psychiatric training he wasn't any more sure than anybody else that I wasn't kidding him about my loss of memory. He was looking for a guilt-reaction that would tell him I already knew what he was going to say.

I grinned. "Well, if I go into shock, this is a good place for it, isn't it?"

He smiled thinly. "Very well, Mr. Madden. You might, in your idle moments, try to recall how you acquired three submachinegun bullets in your right shoulder and arm not too terribly long ago, say within the past two years."

I won't say I hadn't noticed the scars, or the faint residual stiffness in the mornings, but I hadn't given them

27

any thought. Perhaps I'd deliberately avoided thinking about them. I could see why Dr. Lilienthal found the human mind a fascinating subject.

"You're sure?" I asked.

"Fairly sure," Lilienthal said. "Dr. DeLong has had considerable experience in military situations. He says he would wager a tidy sum on their being projectiles from a machine pistol, although two achieved total penetration and the third has been removed. Probably 9mm. They could have come from a 9mm handgun, but something about the grouping seems to indicate a fully automatic weapon to Dr. DeLong. Not a rifle. Three bullets from a highpowered rifle in that large a caliber would pretty well have torn your arm off."

I said, "According to my fiancee, I'm supposed to have spent some time in Vietnam with my cameras."

"Of course, Mr. Madden."

I looked at him sharply. "You have a very unconvincing way of agreeing with a guy, Doc."

Lilienthal said dryly, "You're a very unconvincing guy, Mr. Madden."

"Spell it out, please."

He came back to his chair, swung it around so he could straddle it, and faced me over the back of it. "Let me put it this way," he said. "Do you really *feel* that you are a gentle photographer chap currently specializing in beautiful pictures of little birds and animals?"

I grinned. "At the moment, I'm gentle as a lamb, but the answer to your question is that I'm not sure how I feel. Not yet. Go on."

"The fact is that you have altogether too many marks of violence on your body for a peaceloving cameraman, or even a news photographer with a penchant for trouble. The shoulder wounds are the most recent but there are others. And the most interesting thing about them is that some have been carefully erased, as well as could be managed with plastic surgery, as if somebody'd been interested in making sure you wouldn't cause too much comment with your shirt off."

"So that's it!" I couldn't help laughing. "I thought those investigators from your MOT eyed me very suspiciously, not to mention that closemouthed gent from the RCMP. I suppose this was called to their attention."

Lilienthal looked slightly embarrassed. "As a matter of fact, it was. A doctor has a duty to his patient, but he also has a duty to society. There was no way for us to be certain that the identification found on you wasn't forged or stolen."

"So somebody decided they'd dredged up a professional syndicate hitman, or maybe a soldier of fortune, disabled while engaged in a nefarious operation of some kind, is that it?" I laughed again. "How did you get around the fact that I'd been positively identified by Kittty Davidson. . . . Oh, of course, she was my gun moll helping to preserve my cover. Cover? That's the word, isn't it, Doctor?"

Lilienthal smiled. "Well, some fairly melodramatic theories were considered, I'll admit, although the RCMP quickly determined that Miss Davidson was precisely who and what she claimed to be. Your history was a little harder to obtain, since you are not a Canadian citizen."

"And?"

"Your fingerprints were finally identified in Washington."

I said, "The suspense is awful. I can hardly stand it, Dr. Lilienthal."

He said, "Your fingerprints were positively identified as belonging to Paul Horace Maddén, a reputable photographer with no recorded involvement with the law."

I drew a long breath, not all for display. "Well, if they'd found anything else, that Mountie would be parked outside the door, wouldn't he? What about my fascinating scars?"

"You were severely wounded in Vietnam. It was some time after that—after convalescence—that you began concentrating on peaceful wildlife photography."

There was a little silence. I frowned. "So it's all explained very plausibly, but you're not satisfied. What bugs you, Doctor?"

"Bugs?" It was his turn to frown; then he laughed. "Oh, yes, of course. Bugs!" He became sober and intent once more. "I've done my duty to society, Mr. Madden.

Now my duty is to you, my patient. My professional advice is: don't waste time and effort trying to remember something that never happened, regardless of the official records."

I said slowly, "Something like being wounded in Vietnam while heroically snapping pictures under fire?"

"Exactly. Your various scars were caused by different weapons, and incurred at different times, not in a single traumatic wartime experience. Dr. DeLong tried to point this out to the authorities, but you know how they are when they already have a simple solution to a problem. They refuse to let it be complicated by contradictory information." Lillienthal rose, and spoke curtly: "As far as I'm concerned, you're well enough to be released from this hospital. Goodbye, Mr. Madden."

"Doctor," I said, "you're mad about something. What is it?"

He hesitated, and said, "I think you know."

"Sure," I said. "You think I'm a phony but you're not quite sure. Right?"

He didn't speak for a moment. At last he nodded. "As you say, I'm not sure."

I said, "For what it's worth, you have my word that, no matter what kind of a phony I may turn out to be, my amnesia is perfectly genuine."

He hesitated once more. "Good luck, Mr. Madden," he said again, but his voice was friendlier than it had been.

FIVE

They rolled me to the hospital's front door in a wheelchair. After that I was on my own—well, except for Kitty, who seemed to be indulging a highly developed Florence Nightingale complex. She helped me solicitously to the waiting taxi, which took us to the airport by way of a small car ferry. Apparently there's no real estate level enough for a landing strip on that rugged mainland; the Prince Rupert Airport is therefore located on an island across the harbor.

The plane was a goodsized jet, wide open inside and crammed full of tourist-class-sized seats from bow to stern: a giant, airborne commuter bus. We took off on schedule and headed south. There were snowy mountains off to the left of our course. There was a dense, damp-looking wilderness below. Off to the right, the west, was a misty maze of islands and waterways that reminded me of Scandinavia or pictures of Scandinavia, I wasn't quite sure which. I only knew that I associated that kind of rocky, piny archipelago with a different part of the world; but of course you can see practically anything on color TV these days.

I reminded myself that I must have flown over just such country as this—maybe even this particular landscape—within the past few weeks with a guy named Herb Walters, but I still couldn't bring back a thing from that illfated plane ride. As the big jet rumbled southwards, I was aware of an odd and not entirely unpleasant sense of expectation. It wasn't, I realized, that I thought the rest of my memory would return like a sudden gift from heaven the instant I walked through the door of my own house in Bellevue, Wash. It was, instead, that I had a pretty strong hunch it wouldn't. I'd got back all I was going to for the time being. I was going to have to figure things out for myself. To hell with the recalcitrant mental machinery; I'd spent enough time waiting for it to get into a cooperative mood. It was a challenge, let's say. A good man ought to be able to get by in the present without a lot of help from the past. If a newborn baby could do it, dammit, I could.

"Do we have to change for Seattle?" I asked. "Or does this plane go right through?"

"Who's going to Seattle?" Kitty asked. She reached out and squeezed my hand. Apparently I'd been forgiven for my amorous crudities of yesterday. "I'm taking you home with me," she said, smiling.

I said, "That's called kidnaping, ma'am. A capital offense, I do believe."

"You don't really mind, do you, darling? After all, it isn't as if you hadn't stayed in my apartment before; and you need somebody to look after you for a few days, at least."

"Sure," I said. "How's your cooking? I seem to forget."

"Don't worry so much about your memory," she said. "You're going to be just fine."

I wasn't worrying about my memory, but I was wondering a bit about the girl beside me. She still didn't quite add up to her own billing as a bright PR girl and a complaisant mistress, even a mistress with matrimonial ambitions.

Well, she wasn't the only one who didn't quite make sense. The Chinese kid who'd visited me—I reminded myself that Kitty had never bothered to mention her name to me—hadn't been exactly a little jewel of relaxed and logical behavior, either. My impression was that the Chinese could hold grudges as well as anybody or even a little better; yet my cruelly jilted oriental sweetheart had made a special trip five hundred miles north into the Canadian bush just to relieve my poor sick mind of worry, she'd said.

It was mean of me to doubt her, of course, but my poor sick mind couldn't help considering the possibility that, in spite of her pretty pretense of ignorance, she'd heard that I'd lost my memory and come flying up to get some notion of what I actually remembered and what I didn't. This brought up the question of why my recollections, or lack of them, should be of concern to her. Well, she worked for the outfit that had employed the pilot who'd taken me on that last flight. She even admitted to being emotionally involved with the guy. When you buckled down to think about it hard, you arrived at the interesting fact that there was absolutely no proof that Walters was dead. The only guy who was known to have got hurt on that airborne safari was me. Looking at it from this angle, which no one else seemed to be doing, I could see a lot of fascinating possibilities, mostly threatening to my welfare.

I told myself to go back to the start and try to unravel it from there. The start was now—it had to be—the simple and amazing fact, just handed me by Dr. Lilienthal, that my fingerprints had been sent to Washington, D.C., and had been officially identified as those of P. Madden. Yet one of the few things about myself I knew for sure was that I'd been born M. Helm.

I considered the possibility that, at some time in the part of the past that was still missing to me, the true Mr. Helm had switched identities for some reason, probably nefarious. He'd managed the changeover so well that no government files carried anything but the new information on the false Mr. Madden. . . .

No. It wasn't possible, I told myself. It couldn't have been done, not by a lone man covering his own tracks. I'd been a newspaper photographer for several years; I'd driven a car; I'd paid income tax. There would be—there had to be—all kinds of records extant concerning Matthew Helm, boy cameraman. I couldn't actually recall fingerprints being taken, but somewhere along the line I was sure that, in the line of my newspaper business, I'd have needed a government clearance or permit or pass, since New Mexico, I recalled, has always been full of federal installations. My prints would have gone into storage with the rest of my data. There was also a strong possibility of real military service of some kind, although I couldn't remember any. It was simply not possible that my whirls and loops and ridges were not associated, in the official master memory banks, with the name Helm. Yet, when asked, the computer had belched out Madden, complete with non-combatant war wounds.

There was only one conclusion possible. I hadn't been a lone man covering my own tracks. Somebody in Washington with a lot of clout must have had the official electronic brains carefully reprogrammed to say Madden when somebody pushed the Helm button.

Okay. It was clearing up a little. That would be the same somebody, presumably, who'd set me up in Seattle with appropriate business cards, and cameras and darkroom to match, utilizing my genuine photographic experience to bolster a phony identity. Well, nobody'd go to all that trouble to create a dedicated nature photographer called Madden if there wasn't some kind of an important undercover job for him to do, but what job? I grimaced. There was no way of getting at that, for the moment. Or was there.

I frowned. It was a very odd thing when you came to think of it. I'd been comfortably settled in my quiet hospital room resigned to spending at least another week under medical observation—and suddenly the phone had started ringing with mysterious calls, mysterious visitors had come sneaking through the door, and the doctors who'd been coyly parrying my questions about when they planned to let me go had suddenly fallen all over themselves to get rid of me.

What else had happened? Nothing much. Somebody had just gone and blown up a ferry, that was all. . . .

Kitty put her hand on my knee. "You're not supposed to make faces like that," she said. "You know the doctors told you not to try too hard to remember. . . . What were you trying to remember?"

I said, "Something you've been keeping from me. Sally Wong. She came to see me yesterday."

Kitty took her hand away. "Oh, the little Chinese girl."

"Yeah," I said, "the little Chinese girl I seem to have ditched to get engaged to you. You might have told me. I had to ask her who she was. She wasn't at all sure I wasn't playing some kind of a nasty joke on her. You can hardly blame her."

Kitty laughed, unembarrassed. "Well, what was I supposed to say, that you'd been doing your best for interracial relations when we met, but then you couldn't resist my enchanting personality and magnetic physical attraction. . . . I can't tell you everything, darling. Some things you're just going to have to discover for yourself." She leaned forward a bit so she could see past me, out the plane window. "Look, we're almost there."

Vancouver was a spectacular city surrounding a big harbor and backed by tall white mountains. Actually, the metropolis below seemed to be half water; long fingers ran inland from the open straits over which we flew. The names Burrard Inlet, False Creek, and Fraser River came to me without my being able to recall how or when I'd learned them. The airport was located out on the flat delta of the Fraser, quite a distance south of town. Since we had no luggage to retrieve from the baggage-handling area—I had only the clothes Kitty had brought me plus a small flight bag with my toothbrush and pajamas; and she carried a single case small enough to fit under the airplane seat—we were soon riding away in a taxi.

"The Vancouver Hotel, please," Kitty said to the driver as she settled herself beside me with her big leather purse in her lap. She glanced at me and explained: "We have to pick up my car. I just hated to leave the poor little thing standing at the airport all that time, so I parked it in the hotel garage and took the regular limousine out."

The streets were wet with recent rain, but the sun was shining for a change. It was a fairly long drive involving some big bridges. The clear, bright day made all my elaborate logic seem very shaky, for some reason. After all I was just a guy with a sore head who'd lost a sizeable hunk of his past. Why try to kid myself I could figure it out? The idea that my situation could be in some way related to that bomb on the ferry I'd only read about, well, how farfetched could you get? And that powerful mystery-man I'd dreamed up who'd carefully covered my tracks in Washington. . . .

Kitty reached out and covered my hand with hers. "You're doing it again," she scolded me. "Stop it! Just forget about remembering, dear, and tell me about dinner. I can thaw some nice salmon for you, and I've still got a bottle of that funny Australian wine you liked, but if you're too tired for a real meal just tell me and I'll think of something simple and easy."

"No, that sounds great." I was looking out the cab window as we drove. "You know, it all looks familiar, somehow. The Vancouver Hotel? That's the big, old-fashioned one in the middle of town—Burrard and Georgia Streets, right? The funny thing is, I can see it but I can't see myself seeing it, if you know what I mean. It's just as if I'd read about it in a guidebook."

"Down, Rover, down!" she said, laughing. "Now, for dessert there's French vanilla ice cream with my special homemade sauce to get the last taste of that hospital food out of your mouth. Also, I think, just a touch of that Mexican liqueur you brought me last summer. Kahlua?"

I knew that Kahlua was kind of brownish and tasted like sticky-sweet alcoholic coffee; but of course I couldn't recall bringing it to her. Obviously, however, I'd made quite a production of playing the ardent swain. Yet if I was a man on a secret mission operating under a carefully constructed alias, as everything indicated, it seemed unlikely that my amours, oriental or occidental, would be totally unrelated to my assignment, whatever it was. Nobody'd go to all that trouble to establish an agent in the rainy Northwest just so he could exercise his virility on a pair of irrelevant females. . . .

Kitty said, "Darling, when we get to the hotel, please do exactly as I tell you. Please?"

There was something odd and strained about her voice. I glanced at her quickly. She'd taken a small, nickel-plated, automatic pistol from her purse and she was pointing it straight at me.

SIX

It was terrible treachery, no doubt, and I suppose I should have been shocked and grieved by the dastardly betrayal, but it wasn't as if I'd been taking the girl at face value, and there were too many other things to think about. I remembered that we'd been subjected to no anti-hijack precautions at the little Prince Rupert Airport, so she'd have had no problems there. I stared at the gun. Rather to my surprise, the mental computer kicked out the data: Astra Constable, self-cocking, external hammer, caliber .380 ACP. The letters stood for Automatic Colt Pistol, the now-discontinued weapon for which the cartridge had originally been designed. And the plating wasn't nickel, I corrected myself, it was chrome.

The disturbing thing was that, in addition to knowing exactly what the firearm was, I also knew exactly what to do about it, although it wasn't the kind of knowledge you'd expect from a respectable photographic character named Madden. Presumably the information came from the sinister and shadowy Helm—Dr. Jekyll and Mr. Hyde move over, please. I could see that the girl didn't really want to shoot. I was aware, somehow, that that was all the edge I needed. It would give me an essential fraction of a second. All the moves were clear in my mind. I knew they could work. I knew I could take her, deal with the cab driver as necessary, and get the hell away. . . .

But get the hell away where? And do what when I got there? Well, I did have one other contact with the unremembered part of my past aside from a voice on the phone I had as yet no way of tracing. Sally Wong could still, presumably, be found behind the ticket counter at that waterfront airline, North-Air, and the address was presumably in the phone book—but reason warned me that the neighborhood of Herbert Walters' pretty Chinese playmate might not be a very safe refuge for me in my hour of need. I had no safe refuge, or if I did, I didn't know about it. And safe refuges weren't exactly what I was after, I realized, when I stopped to analyze my own feelings.

I was aware of a funny, nagging, little sense of professional pride, even though I didn't know exactly what my profession was. After all, somebody'd gone to a lot of trouble to send me here, and keep me here for six months. Then something had gone wrong. I must have goofed in some way, since it was unlikely I'd been supposed to wind up in the ocean with amnesia. Now I could either compound the goof by running like a rabbit the first time somebody waved a gun at me, or I could play along with this lovely, amateurish, double-crossing chick and her silly firearm, and learn a few things like where she was planning to take me and who'd be there to greet me.

She was, after all, the best contact I had with my lost past. Everything indicated that I'd gone to a lot of trouble to make her acquaintance; furthermore, it didn't seem likely that she was going to all this trouble just to have me killed. Away from her, not knowing what it was all about, I'd be a blind man trying to find a book in a library he didn't know in order to read the print he couldn't see. . . .

I saw sudden apprehension in Kitty's eyes. "No, Paul! Don't do anything . . . anything rash. Please!"

She was way behind the times. The decision had been made.

"It's your party, Kitty, darling," I said, relaxing beside her. "Your party, complete with my funny Australian wine and your special ice cream sauce."

She looked hurt. "Don't!" she pleaded. "Please don't be angry. You . . . you don't understand. We're not going to hurt you. We're just going to . . . to detain you a little while for your own protection, your own good. Please try to understand!"

I noticed that she kept her voice low, as well as her gun. Apparently the taxi driver was not an accomplice. He jockeyed the cab through the dense downtown traffic, unaware of the drama—or melodrama—behind him. Presently he turned into a narrow driveway between two tall buildings and pulled up at the hotel's rear door, complete with a uniformed doorman, who stepped forward to let us out, and to lift our scanty luggage out of the trunk of the taxi. Kitty maneuvered to stay behind me. The little Astra was out of sight, but her hand was hidden in her purse.

"Pay the nice man, darling," she said, and I got rid of some Canadian bills that, although dry now, hadn't been improved by being thoroughly soaked in sea water not too long ago, along with the other contents of my wallet. I tipped the doorman lightly and picked up the bags. Kitty said, "Let's go inside for a drink first, dear; it's a long drive home," but that was just for public consumption. Once we were inside the high, oldfashioned lobby she said, "No, just walk straight through to the front, please."

I was very much aware of her walking beside me as we marched past the lounge and the desk. I was very glad that the Astra was a double-action-type weapon that, uncocked, took a long, strong pull on the trigger for the first shot. I didn't feel she really knew what she was doing with it—which made her, of course, twice as dangerous as if she had known.

"Right through the front door and across the sidewalk," she said.

Out of the corner of my eye I could see that her face was pale and shiny with strain. I'd have been happier if she hadn't taken it quite so hard. She was tense enough to blow me to hell by mistake and have regretful hysterics afterwards. With a bag in each hand, deliberately handicapping myself to reassure her, I shouldered my way through the big doors, to see a wide, busy street outside. As if on signal, a black Mercedes sedan pulled up at the curb. The rear door opened and a beefy, dark-haired man got out. He was wearing a shabby, dark suit that didn't go with fifteen thousand dollars' worth of vehicle; and a black turtlenecked sweater. His hand was in the pocket of his jacket.

He said, "In the front, Miss. Quick, we're holding up traffic. You, throw that gear on the floor and get in back!"

A moment later we were driving away. The dark-haired man, who'd got in beside me, took his hand from his pocket and displayed a snubnosed Colt revolver in a casual way as if he thought I might be mildly interested. The man behind the wheel was wearing a chauffeur's cap. He seemed to be another beefy muscleman; his neck was broad and red. Kitty, in the other front seat, drew a deep breath, as if happy to be relieved of responsibility. She unbuttoned her long, pink coat. Throwing it wide open for air, she let herself slump down in the seat in an exhausted way, as if she'd run a hard mile on a hot day. For her, I gathered, betrayal was hard work.

"Were you followed from the airport, Miss?" the man beside me asked.

"I . . . I don't know for sure. I didn't want to keep looking around."

He said, "It's practically a dead cert you were, but I think you lost them at the hotel. We'll check. Incidentally, I'm Dugan and that's Lewis. Miss Davidson, isn't it? And this is Mr. Madden, is it, returned from the dead? We want to hear all about that, don't we, Miss Davidson?"

Kitty licked her lips and didn't look at me. "I don't. . . . I wasn't told why. . . . I was promised he wouldn't be hurt."

"Oh, we wouldn't dream of it, Miss," Dugan said. "Gentle as lambs we are. Never lay a finger on him, not a finger."

Kitty stared straight ahead through the windshield. After a little, she organized the bunched pink slacks more becomingly about her legs, and then drew her coat close about her once more as if suddenly chilled. It was another long ride, at least as long as that from the airport. The driver, Lewis, did some early twisting and

40

turning that increased the mileage considerably; but at last, apparently satisfied that there was nobody behind us, he took us out onto a freeway and started making reasonable time. I didn't like the fact that I'd been given the names, and that I wasn't blindfolded. It seemed to indicate that they didn't care what I told, later, which didn't seem likely; or that they didn't figure I'd be in any condition to tell, later. I wondered if I'd made a serious miscalculation when I passed up the chance to escape.

Presently we left the freeway. We were out in the British Columbia countryside now, driving past soggy fields and woodlots drained by deep ditches and creeks running with brown water. The clouds had pulled together once more; the brief moment of sunshine was only a shining memory. The driver turned the Mercedes into a lane that led back between two fenced fields—high, barbed-wire-topped, chain-link fences, I noted—to some white buildings among the trees. We passed a small, neat sign: INANOOK SANITARIUM.

I wondered idly if that was a genuine aborigine name or if somebody was being cutiepie and hinting that this sprawling place was a cozy nook. Except for the institutional white paint, it looked like one of the resort hotels where the guests inhabit expensive individual cottages and bungalows scattered widely around the main building—except that these bungalows, I saw, had bars on the windows. The headquarters structure was impressively large and two stories high. In front of the door, three people awaited us, two men and a woman, all in similar starched white coats. The legs were dressed differently, however. One of the men wore dark trousers. The woman had on practical dull nylons and sturdy brown shoes. The second man wore white starched pants to match his jacket. He was young and blond, with a face that could have been called handsome in its dull and fleshy way. He had big shoulders and muscular hands. He stepped forward as we approached.

"Be nice now," said the man beside me, Dugan. "See, you're getting the VINP treatment. Very Important New Patient. Show your appreciation by not giving us any trouble . . ." The car stopped. He opened the door.

41

"Watch him, Tommy," he said to the big, blond young man. "He's being too good. Don't trust him. All right, Madden, out."

I got out. The two men placed themselves strategically on either side of me. It was clear that, from long practice, they had it all worked out how they'd grab me if grabbing was required; but for the moment they let me stand there untouched. We waited for the man in the dark pants and the woman in the thick nylons. I had a moment to think, which was just as well, since I had to decide just how much warning, if any, I owed these people—and if that sounds strange, it was. I didn't really know what it meant. I just knew it was something I had to do; or not do. It wasn't something that could be let go by default.

Then they were standing in front of me. The man was tallish, although he missed my six-four by several inches. He had a distinguished, professional, gray-at-the-temples look. The woman was the ugliest human female I'd seen in my life—well, as far as I could remember, which wasn't very far. It wasn't that she was seriously deformed in the body. She had all the normal limbs and they all seemed to work. Her legs were ordinary middleaged female legs, not good, not bad. Her hands were perfectly functional human hands. But her face was a collection of bony features out of a scare-the-kids comic book, with a spade chin and a misshapen nose displaying large bulldog nostrils. Under the massive eyebrow ridges, however, the brown eyes were cool and intelligent and dangerous.

"This is Dr. Elsie Somerset, Paul." Kitty had got out beside me to perform the introductions. "And Dr. Albert Caine. . . . They'll take very good care of you, darling. You really shouldn't be out of the hospital so soon; you're much better off. . . ."

I said, "Kitty, why don't you turn off the bullshit?" She gasped and was silent. I looked at Dr. Elsie Somerset—Elsie, for God's sake! I'd made my second big decision for the day. I was going to give them the breaks, silly though it might seem; I was going to give them a chance to back away unharmed. After all, they were only amateurs and I was a pro. Somehow, I was quite sure, now, that I was a pro, even though I didn't know exactly what I was professional at. I asked, "Are you the manager of this funny farm, Dr. Somerset?"

The tall man beside her cleared his throat. "I am the director of this institution, Mr. Madden."

I said, "Fine. Then I'll direct my protest at you. I'd like to state that I've been brought here against my will. I want to leave. I want to go home to Seattle. Okay?"

The two men surrounding me, if you can be surrounded by two men, didn't move, but I could feel them kind of bracing themselves for action.

"I'm afraid that isn't possible, Mr. Madden," said Dr. Caine smoothly. "You've been brought here for treatment—"

"On whose authority?"

"Miss Davidson—"

"The hell with Miss Davidson," I said. "We may or may not be engaged to be married, but even if we are that's hardly a binding legal relationship unless she wants to sue me for breach of promise. I doubt very much that it gives her the right to have me committed to a booby hatch; and where are the commitment papers or whatever the legal equivalent is here in Canada? Let's see something signed by a judge or somebody empowering you to hold me here."

It was play-acting in a way, of course; but there were no longer any guns in sight, and the stuffed shirt in front of me obviously liked to put on a show of legality, even when he was kidnaping perfectly normal strangers off the streets. If I could be considered perfectly normal.

Caine said quickly, "The papers are being drawn up, Mr. Madden. And I would like you to understand that this is an institution of mental healing, not a funny farm or . . . or a booby hatch!"

I said, "Swell, draw up your papers and serve them on me. In Seattle, U.S.A. In the meantime, I'll take my leave, thanks. I won't bother your driver. That's a busy highway out there. I guess it won't take me too long to hitch a ride back to the airport."

I turned. The two men grabbed for me. Again, as with Kitty and her gun, I could see with almost frightening clarity how to handle it: first crippling one and then turning to deal with the other, but that wasn't the point of the exercise. I therefore just swung a clumsy fist at the dark one, and he got mad and slammed me alongside the head so I fell down. I heard a slight murmur of protest from the blonde one. Okay, that was something learned. They took me by the arms and hauled me back to a standing position.

Breathless, and a little dazed by the blow, I looked at Kitty. "Let's hear it again, doll. Nobody was going to hurt me, remember? Socking the head of a guy just recovering from concussion doesn't count, huh?"

"Oh, I told you not to do anything—"

"Sweetie," I said, "considering the painless reception I'm getting outside, I can hardly wait to see what treatments I'm due for inside." Before she could speak, I looked at the two doctors and said, "We've now established clearly that I'm being kept here by force, against my will, right?" A little uneasiness flickered in the man's pale gray eyes, but the woman's brown eyes just looked faintly amused by the antics of the laboratory specimen impaled on the pin. Kitty looked thoroughly miserable. There was something I needed to know. Considering that I'd been brought here at gunpoint, it was a ridiculous question to ask, but I asked it anyway: "Okay, if you won't let me leave, how about letting me make a phone call?"

"I'm sorry, that isn't possible—"

Dr. Caine's smooth voice was interrupted by a hoarse question from the woman: "Whom do you want to call, Mr. Madden?"

Acromegaly was the word, I remembered. It gives them that kind of voice in addition to the other deformities. The pituitary gland goes haywire, I believe, but you'd better look it up for yourself if you're really interested.

"That's my business," I said, but I had my answer. Actually, of course, I had no idea whom to call, but Kitty had looked uneasy. Obviously there was somebody

44

I could call and she knew about it. All I had to do was find out the identity and phone number. "What about it?" I asked the lady doctor. "One phone call? It's mandatory in the States before you're thrown in jail."

The gentleman doctor winced. "Mr. Madden, please! This is *not* a jail—"

The woman said, "Never mind, Albert. This man is merely playing games with us. The other patients have seen enough of their new fellow-inmate; now bring him inside and we'll run him through the rest of the routine for their benefit." She glanced at the driver. "Oh, Gavin, take Miss Davidson home and stand by. I may want to send for you later this evening."

"Yes'm," said Lewis.

"All right, Dugan, Trask, bring him along."

"Dr. Somerset," I said.

"What is it now?"

She was a bright woman, but she didn't understand. I felt obliged to make a final try at explaining it to her. "I'd like to make a point, if it isn't clear already," I said. "To me, you're kidnapers. In my country, kidnaping is a capital offense, and I don't suppose they smile on it here in Canada."

"Yes, yes," she said impatiently, "I'm sure the presiding judge will order us all hanged in a row, like apples on a tree, Mr. Madden. Now come along, please."

I felt better. It hadn't been the best move in the world, strategically speaking. It would have been better to keep a low profile, as they say, from the very beginning. However, I'd discharged my obligation to them, all of them. Whatever happened now, my conscience was clear; and I could start lowering the profile inch by inch until they forgot the little glimmer of resistance I'd shown on arrival and considered me absolutely harmless.

The only trouble was, they might be right. I wouldn't really know how harmless I was, or wasn't, until the time came.

SEVEN

As I was being marched up the steps to the front door by my two-man escort, I was aware of Kitty getting back into the Mercedes. Her troubled face appeared at the window, looking my way pleadingly. It was too bad. I mean, a girl ought to get a big bang out of her betrayals, or why bother? I decided she wasn't the girl I really wanted to marry, after all.

"This way, Mr. Madden."

It was Dr. Somerset's hoarse voice; and I followed the woman through the door and into the headquarters building. There was a spacious, hotel-type lobby in which several people were sitting, some in sports clothes, some in pajamas and dressing gowns. They looked bored and dull and not particularly insane. My hunch was that they were well-paying patients who'd come here to find temporary refuge from the bottle or the needle under medical supervision. Aside from the invalid-type costumes of some of the guests, the only thing out of the ordinary was a kind of discreet sentry-box just inside the door in which a uniformed, armed guard was lounging. I realized that, the way the fences were arranged, coming right up to the house, this front door was the only visible exit from the place. You'd have to get by the security man and then make a quarter-mile sprint down the long lane to the highway, with no assurance that somebody would stop and pick you up when you got there.

Well, I'd already passed up an opportunity to get away, and a quarter-mile dash was beyond me, anyway. I was aware that the trip had already taken most of my limited strength, and that if a crisis arose involving physical effort it would be just too damned bad. The inmates watched us dully as we crossed the lobby.

"Our dining room and kitchen are over there." Dr. Somerset leading the way, made a gesture with her hand, obviously speaking for our uninterested audience. "I think you'll find our food first class, Mr. Madden, although you'll be eating it in your quarters for the time being. . . . This way, please."

It was a large office. I was led through it to an examining room with the usual stainless steel table, with cabinets full of medical-looking bottles and jars along the walls. Obeying instructions, I stripped to my shorts and submitted to a thorough physical examination while one of the guards—the other had vanished—stood at the door to see that I behaved myself. He was Dugan, the darker and meaner-looking of the two. I was happy to note that he had to keep dabbing at a cut lip, where my deliberately inexpert swing had connected. It occurred to me that I didn't seem to be a very charitable person, basically. Well, I suspected that my situation was one in which I wouldn't find charity very helpful.

Dr. Somerset wrote down my height, weight, pulse rate, blood pressure, and various other vital statistics. She looked down my throat and up my rear in the way of doctors everywhere. After the time I'd just spent being cared for like a baby by the nurses in the Prince Rupert Hospital, being examined by a lady doctor didn't bother me a bit. Finally, I was allowed to dress. Then I was taken back into the outer office and parked in a chair while Dr. Somerset seated herself behind the gray metal desk and made some final notes on my case—obviously, if anybody came looking they'd find that that poor, unfortunate lunatic, Paul Horace Madden, had received precisely the same processing as any other sanitarium patient. At last the woman looked up deliberately.

"Mr. Madden," she said, "you were kind enough to make it clear that to you I'm a kidnaper and a criminal. Therefore let me now make it clear that to me you're a perfectly sane man with a perfectly good memory. From time to time I'll ask you for information. You're entitled to refuse to give it. If I find it necessary, I'll try to persuade you to change your mind by various means, but I won't hold your refusal against you. I do not, however, like to be taken for a fool. Forget what you told those idiots at the hospital. I don't want to hear the word amnesia. Answer my questions or don't answer them, but don't say you don't remember. That response will not be accepted, Mr. Madden. Do you understand?"

It was an interesting approach; and obviously we'd finished with the phony doctor-patient routines. I wondered if she really meant it or if she was running a bluff. Either way, the results were likely to be painful.

"When does the game start?" I asked.

She frowned. "What do you mean?"

"Are we playing under those rules right now?" I asked. "I don't want to incur an unnecessary crack on the head for breaking them."

She hesitated. "Let's say the rules don't apply yet. Why?"

"I just wanted to get it on record that you're wrong, Dr. Somerset. Unless you've got some very good tricks in your back room—I suppose there's a back room full of tricks in this place—you're not going to get anything out of me about a certain period of my life, not unless your tricks are good enough to let *me* get through to what's missing. I don't know what's there myself, so I can't tell you about it. A little early stuff has come back, but there's still no recent material in sight. Unless you've got something that'll let me break through into the storage vault, you'll be wasting your time asking questions about it."

"I have plenty of time. I don't mind wasting a little."

"Sure," I said. It was no use, but I had to keep trying. Something might register that would save me suffering later. I went on: "It's what you'll be doing while you're wasting that time that bothers me, Doctor. I may not know exactly who I am, but I do know I'm no hero. Please get that straight. I'm not about to suffer in stoical silence if I can help it. Any answers I've got, you've got. All you have to do is ask. Don't go haywire with a lot of scientific tortures just because you refuse to recognize

48

the truth, which is that I simply can't remember certain things."

The woman's eyes narrowed. "Tortures? Who said anything about tortures, Mr. Madden? And what does a respectable photographer know about tortures, anyway?"

"Nuts," I said. "Your boy Dugan isn't exactly close-mouthed; he likes a spot of menace. And he brought me here with a gun. I was knocked down when I tried to leave. I've just been told that if I refuse to answer questions you'll try to persuade me to change my mind. Persuade! Any TV-watcher worth his salt knows what that means, particularly in a place like this. How stupid am I supposed to be?"

She studied me carefully for a moment. I'd made a small impression. Maybe I'd even implanted a seed of doubt. It was all I could hope for.

"Who's Helm?"

The question caught me by surprise. "What?"

The woman was leaning forward across the desk, still watching me closely. "You just said you'd give me all the answers you had. Somebody called you at the hospital and used that name. Tell me about it."

I grimaced. "So my room and phone were bugged? That explains a few things." I shrugged. "I can't tell you who Helm is, but I'm Helm."

"Explain."

"Let's put it this way," I said carefully. "A bit of ancient history returned, maybe as a direct result of hearing that name. I now know that I was a kid named Matthew Helm going to school during the week and hunting with his daddy on weekends. That I remember. Then I remember being a young fellow named Helm taking pictures for various newspapers. Then there's a long hiatus. Then I woke up in a hospital and was told that I'm now a dedicated nature photographer named Madden recuperating from a terrible flying accident. I don't remember anything about that. Aside from minor details, which I'll happily supply without coercion, that's all you're going to get if you work on me a week, because that's all there is to get, Doctor."

She asked flatly, as if she hadn't really been listening: "Where's Walters?"

There it was, the bad news Dugan had hinted at, confirmed. If they were interested in Pilot Walters' last flight, if that was what the whole thing was all about, I was in for a very unhappy time.

I said, "I was told that Herbert Walters, known as Herb, worked for an outfit known as North-Air. I was told that he'd flown me north in a DeHaviland Beaver. I was told that I'd flown with him before. I was told that he's still missing, along with his plane. Presumably, he sank with the plane, but of course he could have parachuted clear, earlier, and left me to crash alone. I simply don't know."

"Walters is very important to us. We have to know what happened to Mr. Herbert Henry Walters."

She didn't say who had to know and it didn't seem diplomatic to ask. I just shrugged helplessly. "If I knew I'd tell you."

"You do know."

I said, "Well, okay, maybe I do know, in the technical sense. Maybe it's up there somewhere with the stored memory tapes. But I can't get at it."

She nodded slowly. "We'll see, Mr. Madden. We'll see what you can get at." She looked towards Dugan. "All right, take him to Hyacinth. Tell Tommy Trask maximum security at all times. . . . Oh, just a minute. Mr. Madden, let me show you something before you go. In here."

I rose and followed her through the examining room I'd already seen. She opened a heavy, sound-proof door beyond, and there it was again: more bad news I'd been expecting. I won't even bother to describe it, except to say that this was a modern installation with no racks or thumbscrews or Iron Maidens on display. I gathered that the work was done largely by electricity. There was a chair into which you could be strapped, or they could stretch you out on a table for better accessibility. Bodybelts. Wrist and ankle straps. There was a faint odor. I could be fancy and call it the smell of pain, but actually the joint smelled more like a public john.

"So this is the fun room," I said.

Dr. Somerset let the heavy door hiss closed behind us. "The rules are now in force, Mr. Madden, so consider your future answers very carefully. . . . All right, Dugan. Take him to Hyacinth and turn him over to Tommy."

"Yes, ma'am." Dugan gave me a shove. "Not that way. The back door, over in the corner. . . ."

There was Aster, Buttercup, Columbine, Dahlia, and so on down to Goldenrod and Hyacinth. I mean, so help me, that's what the damned, barred, loony-bin cottages were named. I found that almost as frightening as the room I'd just seen.

EIGHT

Actually, it wasn't so bad, or maybe I should say it was bad but I wasn't in good enough shape to appreciate it. You'd think a sick man—well, a man just recovering from sickness—would be easier to break down than a well one, but this time, at least, it worked the other way. I still hadn't come back to full reality after my recent brush with death. This was just one more chapter in a long, hazy, continuing hospital nightmare, and I was getting pretty hardened to hazy hospital nightmares.

They let me think it over for a whole night and day, plus one more night. I spent most of that time in bed, mostly sleeping. Any fool could figure out what was going to happen when they started asking me urgent questions about an airplane jockey I couldn't remember. Why borrow trouble by brooding about it in advance?

The second evening, the buildup started. They prepared me as if for an operation: the clean-you-out pills, the nothing-to-eat-and-drink edict, and in the morning, further unpleasant precautions against my messing up their pretty torture chamber under stress, followed by a shot. In a real hospital, it would have been a preliminary sedative or anesthetic, but here I thought it was probably a cooperation injection of some kind. Scopolamine? The word popped into my mind from somewhere, but I rejected it. It was my impression—gained where, I didn't know—that scopolamine was considered pretty corny and old-fashioned nowadays. A place like this probably had better truth juices available.

Dr. Caine administered the injection. I was put into

a wheelchair—the blond orderly named Trask did the honors here—and rolled to the main building, where Dugan opened the back door to admit us to the Torquemada room. I'd seen a few people, well bundled up, strolling aimlessly under the trees of the big fenced estate. They'd paid no attention to me. Maybe I wasn't really there at all, I reflected; maybe I was back in the Prince Rupert Hospital having a highly colored dream. Here I was being transported quite openly to the chamber of horrors, and none of my fellow-patients would even acknowledge my existence by a glance. Actually, I had a hunch they were quite aware of me; they simply didn't want to seem rudely curious about the poor violent case locked up in high-security Hyacinth, now scheduled for desperate treatments to restore his sanity. I mean, it would have been impolite to stare, don't you know?

Trask turned me over to Dugan, who rolled me inside to where the horror lady herself awaited me. Dr. Albert had faded at the door; apparently he was okay with the needle but he had no stomach for the heavy work with the electrodes and rheostat. We started in the chair with questions. We continued in the chair with electricity. Then the electric treatments were continued on the table, with interesting variations. As I said, I was pretty used to institutional nightmares by now. I knew how to escape them. All I had to do was move off into a corner of the room and watch the fun. I was acquainted with the guy in the chair, or on the table, and I thought they were treating him badly and it was a real shame, but when you came right down to it he wasn't a fellow who meant a great deal to me. . . .

I was a little startled, maybe even a little scared, when I suddenly realized somewhere along the line that this was no longer the first day of intermittent questioning, it was the second. I'd lost a day. Well, it seemed to be something I was getting good at, mislaying memories. I didn't think the ones I'd misplaced inside that room were anything I'd miss. I stopped worrying about it once I decided that the mental circuit breakers, the ones that cut out during psychic overloads like airplane crashes, were simply doing their protective stuff once more, shutting out a lot of stuff I didn't really want.

I did worry a bit about the Observer, as I called him. He was a small fat man with a surgeon's mask and cap and gown who stayed in the corner so unobtrusively it had taken me a while to realize he was there. He didn't act much like a surgeon. In fact he didn't act at all. Elsie carried out the treatments, with the help of Dugan's muscle when required. The Observer simply observed. Once in a very long while he'd make a comment. He had a pleasant enough voice, in spite of a Germanic accent, and sometimes what he said was pleasant, too. At least I found it so.

"No, no," he'd say, "We can't have him dead or permanently damaged, Dr. Somerset. You'd better let him rest a bit now, *hein?*"

In a way, however, I resented his presence. Somehow it wouldn't have been so bad with just me and Elsie— and Dugan, but he didn't really count, he was just the eunuch at the harem door. We worked out a very satisfactory love-hate relationship as the inquisition progressed, Elsie and I. I was her pet toy, and she was somebody I was going to kill very slowly, very deliberately, very painfully, when *my* time came. The ingenious torments I devised for her—to hell with simple electricity —kept me going during the times when the drugs wore thin and the disinterested-spectator technique didn't quite work any longer. But having an observer present during out intimate orgies of pain wasn't right, I felt. It was like making love in public, dammit.

"That's enough, I think," said the Observer one day, coming forward. It was the first time he'd left his corner station while I was in the room. He went on, "That is enough, Madame Doctor. I think we can take it as established that the man has actually lost his memory, *nicht wahr?* Furthermore it's becoming quite obvious that we won't break through to the information we need by these methods. There is nothing to be gained by proceeding further."

"If you'd only let me—"

Elsie's voice was even hoarser than usual with disappointment. She was an ugly, lonely little girl being

54

told to stop playing with her favorite doll. I almost felt sorry for her.

"No. He must live and he must recover, those are my instructions." The masked little man's voice was sharp. "The name he gave you, the name spoken over the telephone, has been traced. We have some very interesting, but rather disturbing, information about this man and the organization for which he works. He is really a very interesting person. It's too bad he had to get involved in our affairs. In his business—his real business, which is not photography—occasional interrogations are expected, so I think we need fear no retribution for what we have done so far. There are, however, people behind him who may take action if we go much farther; people it's considered advisable not to antagonize. That telephone call was as much to us as to him. It was a warning. We feel it should be heeded. Let's wrap it up, as the Yankees say. Lock him up and keep him safe until you get further instructions from the council. We'll have to try to learn about Walters some other way."

When the Observer had gone, Elsie herself came forward to release me, although that was normally Dugan's job. She looked at me for a long time, fondly, sadly, before tackling the straps and buckles. I was tempted to congratulate her. Even when it's checked, as seemed to be the case with her, acromegaly usually has unfortunate sexual side effects; but she had obviously made a wonderful adjustment and found a very satisfactory substitute. However, looking up at the intelligent eyes in the gargoyle face, I managed to keep my mouth shut. I'd survived. I knew, at least in part by not fighting or talking back. My profile was nice and low again. No sense in spoiling things by getting smartalecky at the last moment.

Dugan was almost as disappointed as Elsie, I think. He yanked me out of there angrily, rolled me roughly back to Hyacinth, and practically threw me at Tommy Trask.

"The skinny bastard beat them!" Dugan said bitterly. "Him and his phony amnesia! If they'd just let me at that rheostat, I'd have got it out of him in a hurry."

"Or burned out his transistors," Trask said. "Vegetables don't talk. . . . Come on, Mr. Madden, it's time for beddy-bye."

"The orders are to keep him *safe*," Dugan said.

"We're safe, aren't we, Mr. Madden," Trask said. "Safe as a baby in a crib, we are. . . ."

I went to sleep, smiling like a baby in a crib. Phase one had been concluded in a reasonably satisfactory manner, everything considered. It was time for phase two, but there was no hurry, no hurry at all. A little strength and good sense would be required. I slept all the next day, therefore, except for meals. I'd been kept on very short, bland, and unsatisfying rations for obvious reasons connected with sanitation. Now Trask started bringing me real food, and I made up for lost time and calories. Between meals, I slept some more. Gradually, the drugs I'd been given wore off and the haze of pain, illness, and weariness began to clear.

I hadn't paid much attention to the room before, since I wasn't planning to do much about it. I wasn't the Count of Monte Cristo planning to dig his way out of the Chateau d'If; and as I recalled, in the end the guy hadn't made it with a shovel after all. But a little geography wouldn't hurt, and as sharp reality came back to me, I studied my surroundings carefully—it was actually quite a comfortable little suite—determined the way the door locked, and examined the view from the barred windows of the two rooms and adjacent bathroom. I got a pretty good idea of the lay of the land outside: how the cover was located and which way the paved walks ran under the trees.

Trask was a different matter. He was important. I'd been making fuzzy mental notes about Tommy Trask ever since I understood that he'd been assigned to me for the duration. Now I clarified and completed my research on the subject. He was almost six feet tall and he weighed well over two hundred muscular pounds. Even in good health, I would have hesitated to test my strength against his. Like Kitty Davidson, he spoke with that kind of half-British–sounding Canadian accent I could never track to its source. He had longish blond hair and a heavy face that, as I've already indicated, had a hint of handsome boyishness. He wasn't very bright but he wasn't a bad guy. . . .

I didn't know what I was waiting for, really, until that evening came. It felt right, somehow. I wasn't going to get any stronger or smarter cooped up here. If I stalled much longer, something might happen to change my situation for the worse. I heard Trask coming, whistling to himself. It was a roast-beef night, I realized, and he liked being able to bring his private patient something good, unlike last night when the dinner menu had consisted of a mixed-up Chinese-type mess that no self-respecting Oriental would have fed to his cat.

I watched the door open. I stepped back to the window as I was supposed to; we'd settled these small points of discipline long ago, quite amicably. Trask shoved the door wide, checked my location, and turned back to get the tray he'd left on the shelf beside the door so he'd have both hands free in case I had some notion of jumping him as he entered. His expression, as always recently, was slightly apologetic, indicating that he knew these precautions were unnecessary between us, but after all a job was a job and he liked to do it right. He pulled the door closed one-handed, just in case I should take it into my head to make a run for it while he was busy setting out my meal on the little table by the wall. The door could only be opened with a key, from either side. The key was in his pocket.

"A little underdone, just like you like it, Mr. Madden," he said cheerfully as he uncovered the plate. "And I got you a beer. Just a sec while I open it for you. Sorry about the steak knife, but that's a nice tender piece of meat; you'll do all right with your fork."

I grinned, coming forward as he stepped aside. "Sure. Hell, if I had a knife I might cut your throat. You never know with a dangerous character like me. . . . Oh, *damn!*" I'd knocked the bottle off the corner of the table as I seated myself. "Oh, damn it, Tommy, I'm sorry. . . ."

He went for the bottle, which hadn't shattered. It was rolling across the floor spewing beer and foam on the carpet. Bent over to grab it, he stopped abruptly, realizing what he was doing. That was when I hit him and broke his neck.

NINE

I'll have to admit that it surprised me almost as much as it did him. I'd known, somehow, that it could be done that way, but I hadn't had any really good reason to think I could do it. I'd been ready to throw myself on top of him and pin him down and finish him off, one way or another, before he could recover from the first blow. It wasn't necessary. He went down instantly. There were some ugly, convulsive jerks and twitches as the final, fading signals filtered through the damaged circuits; then he lay limp and still.

I rubbed my hand, stinging from the force of the blow. It was badly bruised—apparently I wasn't the brick-smashing type of karate expert—but nothing seemed to be broken. Okay. Keys and a weapon next. I got the keys from his pocket. I was fairly sure, from careful observation, that he carried no armaments, but I searched him anyway. Nothing. He'd been picked for his ability to deal with maniacs barehanded; and in a place like that you don't want to give a maniac an opportunity to become an armed maniac. Only the security guards, the last line of defense so to speak, were permitted firearms on the premises. I took his wallet, since I didn't know where my own had got to, and money might be required if I did manage to get clear of this place. That made me feel a bit guilty, like a thief.

I let myself out of the room, but paused to look back. Something told me that if you can do it you'd damned well better be able to look at it. Poor Tommy. I suppose there are always guys who aren't really bad guys who get themselves stuck on the wrong sides of situations. Maybe it was my imagination but the dead boyish face seemed to have a reproachful expression. Well, hell, I'd warned them, and he'd been right there when I did it. I'd given them a chance to let me leave peacefully, hadn't I? If they persisted in locking people up and running electricity through them after being properly cautioned, they could damned well take the consequences.

Hyacinth Cottage contained my prison suite and a sitting room for the nurse or orderly. Off the sitting room were a small bathroom—just a toilet and basin—and a closet. In the closet I found my clothes and some sanitarium equipment, including several interesting canvas garments well-equipped with straps, and two pairs of crutches, aluminum and wood. Apparently they'd had a crazy cripple to deal with, or expected one. The aluminum tubing was too light for my purposes. I dismantled one of the wooden crutches by removing two wing-nuts and driving out the bolts. I checked the straight lower section after discarding the rubber tip. It seemed to be sound hardwood and it was almost two feet long. It would have to do.

I got dressed. It felt odd to have on real clothes once more, after living so long—with just one brief day's interlude—in pajamas. My overcoat and airplane bag weren't there. I left my sports jacket reluctantly, after checking that it held nothing I'd miss if I couldn't come back. There was nothing in my pants, either. Fortunately, the going-away costume Kitty had provided me in Prince Rupert included a reasonably warm turtle-necked sweater, so going outdoors stripped for action involved no serious risk of pneumonia.

Nevertheless, I shivered as the cold, damp air hit me outside the cottage door. I guess my stint in the cold waters of Hecate Strait had left me with a chronic yearning for warmth and dryness. It was night outside, but they had enough lights on the premises for midnight football. The vague mist seemed to radiate the illumination into all corners that might have sheltered me. To hell with it. I'd be more conspicuous sneaking from one patch of cover to the next than just walking along like a gent on legitimate business. I strolled away casually, therefore, swinging my length of crutch jauntily, like a cane.

It was too late for any patients to be outside. They were either eating in the main dining room or being served in their cottages, depending on medical and psychological condition. For the moment, there were no employees in sight. With Trask eliminated, there was only one employee below the administrative level who concerned me, anyway. The rest had, and apparently wanted to have, nothing to do with the operation of the two Snake Pits, as Goldenrod and Hyacinth seemed to be known: the violent wards. Tommy had told me this resentfully, I remembered. He'd thought it unfair that his fellow-workers considered themselves superior to him just because they dealt with simple lushes and dope fiends instead of. . . .

I saw Dugan coming, carrying a tray. Instinctively, I started to take cover; then I changed my mind. Actually, it was a stroke of luck catching him in the open like this. Otherwise I would have had to worry about him until I found him and immobilized him. Dugan being Dugan —I considered myself a Dugan expert by this time— there were better ways of handling him than jumping out from behind a bush and saying *boo*. I continued to walk towards him.

It was typical of Dugan, I reflected, that he was serving somebody's dinner half an hour late. It was also typical of Dugan that, seeing a patient loose who shouldn't be, he never once thought of raising the alarm. I'd counted on that. He could handle it personally, Dugan could. He needed no help, did Dugan. He set the tray carefully on one of the benches along the path, and kept on coming, reaching behind him. No gun, I hadn't seen any further indications of the compact Colt he'd shown me when we first met, but it was also typical of Dugan, I knew, that he carried something in his hip pocket that wasn't a wallet or a handkerchief, regardless of the house rules.

I'd seen the bulge of it often enough, but I'd never managed to identify it. Now, as he pulled it out, I saw that it was a slim and flexible blackjack of some kind.

Maybe it was what the British call a cosh, but don't ask me where I'd heard that word because I didn't know.

"Where the hell do you think you're going?" Dugan asked as we stopped about ten feet apart. "Where's Tommy?"

"Tommy isn't anywhere," I said. "Not any longer. Poor Tommy."

His face changed. His eyes narrowed oddly. If I'd thought Dugan could feel concern for anybody but himself, I would have said I'd just startled and worried him. Well, I'd wondered a little about the relationship between the two of them; not that their love life was any of my damned business. Dugan spoke harshly, as if to reassure himself.

"You're a bloodly liar. Tommy isn't Einstein, or Muhammed Ali either, but he'd never let you. . . ."

I sighed. "Dugan, you talk too damned much. Are you going to do something with that thing besides slap it against your palm like that, or am I just supposed to fall down dead with fright at the noise?"

He said, "Since you ask for it, cock, it will be a real pleasure."

He came forward in a half-crouch, weaving a bit, feinting with the sap. I brandished my stick clumsily, like a feeble club. He laughed and kept advancing. I struck out at him in an ineffectual way, and jumped back fearfully as he responded with a slash of his own weapon. I stumbled dramatically. He laughed again, and came in like a bear to honey. I arranged my feet properly and drove the stick straight at his eyes, rapier-fashion. A man six-four has considerable range when he extends himself in a full fencing lunge, even with just a two-foot stick. Dugan recoiled; his arms went up to protect his face. Instantly, in mid-lunge, I dropped the point and sent it into his belly with the full weight of my body behind it, trying to remember the Italian name of that high-low attack that I'd first learned, I recalled, on a college fencing team back when I was still just a nice young fellow with photographic ambitions racking up a few points for phys. ed.

I wasn't so young, and I didn't seem to be so nice,

any longer. I heard the breath go out of Dugan. He doubled up helplessly, hugging himself, sinking to his knees. I looked down at him for a moment. I could see no need whatever to take any risks for Dugan's sake, like the risk of leaving him tied up to maybe work himself free and alert the guards before I was ready for them. My right hand was too tender for any further flashy displays of karate, if that was what it was. I stepped behind Dugan, slipped my hands under his armpits, and brought them up and around, locking them together at the nape of his neck and levering his head forward. I remembered the name of that wrestling hold all right: the venerable and respected full nelson. I heard him groan as the pressure came on.

"Goodbye, Dugan," I said. "Don't think it hasn't been nice, because it hasn't."

Afterwards, I dragged him into the nearest ornamental bushes, and liberated his cosh and wallet, and his key ring, heavier than Tommy's. I left him my part-crutch, and got the tray he'd put aside and shoved it in with him to prevent anybody from getting curious about it. Then I frowned thoughtfully, getting curious about it myself. I uncovered the meal on the tray. It was the same kind of bland and uninteresting food, totally digestible and totally lacking in substance, that I'd been getting to keep me alive, just barely, while Dr. Elsie worked on me. I hadn't been aware that another patient was undergoing the same treatment.

I looked around, and crouched quickly in the dripping bushes as a whiteclad figure emerged from a cottage some fifty yards away and headed towards the main building carrying a disheveled-looking tray that had obviously served its nutritional purpose for the time being. I didn't know the name of the cottage, and it didn't concern me, but now I remembered that when I left Hyacinth there had been a light in the neighboring bungalow.

Well, I'd known in a vague sort of way that Goldenrod was occupied but, with troubles of my own, I hadn't spent much time speculating about my next-door neighbor. There was really, I told myself, no reason why I should do so now. The place was lousy with loonies I didn't know and didn't want to know. Dugan's private patient was probably a perfectly legitimate mental case undergoing perfectly legitimate therapy. After all, on a place this size, they couldn't spend all their time tormenting people.

I hesitated, drew a long breath, and went back for a look. Goldenrod Cottage was larger than Hyacinth, and had two detention suites, one at each end. The near one was dark. I slipped along the rear of the building to the lighted, barred, windows. The blind was down, but Dugan had done his usual sloppy job. There was a two-inch gap below one. I peered inside cautiously and saw a thin, plain woman in a soiled hospital gown slumped in a chair in the corner, nobody I'd ever seen before. . . .

Then, looking more closely, I drew a sharp little breath, as I realized that the naked legs were actually quite young and slim and that the figure was youthful, too, although on the slender and economical side of feminine perfection. It was Kitty Davidson.

TEN

It was a complication I didn't need. It confronted me with a decision I had no desire to make, although there was really no reason why I should even hesitate. After all, who was it who'd betrayed me into the hands of Dr. Elsie and Dr. Albert in the first place? Apparently, angry at not getting the information they'd wanted out of me, they were now punishing Kitty for their failure. All I had to do, before proceeding with the business of getting myself out of here, was treat myself to a good look at my sweet female Judas, now hunched there gracelessly in her dirty gown with her dull eyes staring blankly through her straggling hair. It couldn't have happened to a nicer slut, right?

The only trouble was that it didn't really make sense. I didn't get it. If she was on the same side—of what?—as Elsie and Albert, as I'd naturally assumed after the way she'd brought me here, why would they put her through the electric wringer? The familiar red marks of the hold-down straps on her wrists and ankles—mine were still visible, although fading—confirmed what I'd already guessed from the diet she was being fed; but if they were just mad at her for bringing to their nuthouse a pecan they couldn't crack, so to speak, there were much simpler ways for them to show their displeasure. Scientific interrogation suggested that they might have some doubts about her loyalty to them. If she was with them all the way, all they had to do was ask, wasn't it? In any case it indicated that they thought she knew something they didn't. It seemed likely that, in my memoryless state, I'd find the same information useful. I reminded myself that it was fairly certain, at least, that she had a telephone number of some interest to me.

Dugan's keys let me into the building and admitted me to her suite. She didn't hear me open the door, or pretended she didn't. Well, if she thought I was Dugan bringing her tasteless dinner of bouillon and fruit juice there'd be no reason for her to jump up to greet me with instant joy.

"Kitty," I said. She looked around vacantly and stared at me in a puzzled way, as if she wasn't quite certain where she'd seen me before. I felt a sense of loss, remembering the bright, pretty girl I'd known. It was hard to keep a good hate focused on this vague, bedraggled creature. I said deliberately, "You make a great Snake Pit picture, Kitty, darling. Just let a little drool run down your chin now and you'll be perfect."

Her head came up. Her eyes came to life with angry recognition. "Why . . . why you unspeakable *beast*!" she gasped, lunging out of her chair.

I caught her wrists as she came at me. Although I owed her nothing, as far as I knew, but the best part of a week of electronic horror, I was relieved. It was all right. She could get mad and everything. Dr. Elsie hadn't hit the higher numbers on the rheostat. Miss Davidson might be slightly frayed around the edges, but she was still with us.

"Relax, relax," I said, holding her. "I'm sorry, I just had to snap you out of it. Where are your clothes?"

She stopped fighting me and, after I'd released her, frowned at me in a bewildered way. "Did . . . did they let you go? Are they turning us loose?"

"Us?" I said. "What's this *us* bit? Whose side are you on, anyway, Kitty?"

"Why, yours, of course," she said. "I mean—"

"You have a hell of a funny way of showing it."

She flushed. "Oh, I see. Just because I. . . . You think I. . . . Oh, I just can't think clearly!" She swayed, standing there, and I reached out to steady her. "They've got me all mixed up, that horrible woman and her dreadful machine that turns you into a helpless puppet twitching and kicking on a string. . . . Oh, Paul, get me out of here. Please! I can't stand any more of that. I can't *stand* it."

I held her once more, as she started to cry. "It's all right, Kitty."

After a while, she stiffened abruptly in my arms, in a panicky way. "They *didn't* let you go, did they? You escaped! And that awful man Dugan will be coming here any minute with my dinner, he's late already. Quick, we've got to get away before he—"

"Don't worry about Dugan. I've already had a little talk with Mr. Dugan and persuaded him not to bother us." I went on quickly before she could ask questions: "And there are a few things I've got to know before we start running around in the rain. Like, if I'm on your side, why am I here, courtesy of an Astra .380 held by you?"

"Astra?" Her voice was muffled against me. "Oh, the gun."

"Yeah," I said. "The gun."

"I didn't want him to do it," she said, still clinging to me. "I tried to talk him out of it—"

"Who?"

She hesitated. "You're sure Dugan won't. . . . He gives me the creeps; he's almost as bad as that female monster he works for."

"Never mind Dugan. Who told you to turn me over to them?"

"The man in Washington. . . . Can't we talk later? I want to get out of here now!"

"What man in Washington?"

She sniffed loudly. "You know, the one you work for. Oh, of course you don't remember, but you told me to get in touch with him if anything ever happened to you." Another big sniff. "Well, it did, so I did. After your crash I called him at the number you'd given me—"

"What number?"

She told me. I made her repeat it once and said, "Okay, I've got it. What's his name?"

"I don't know his full name. You just called him Mac. Darling, can't we please go now? At least find my clothes so I can be dressing while you—"

I said, "So this Mac I work for had you throw me to the wolves. Nice guy."

She freed herself and stepped back. She spoke breathlessly fast: "He said it was regrettable but unavoidable, and you'd been trained to cope with situations like that. He said it was the only way we'd ever find this place, for me to do exactly as they asked. Otherwise I'd lose their confidence altogether and all our work would be wasted. If . . . if I didn't turn you over to them, if I tried to protect you, they'd know I wasn't a real convert to the great cause for which my husband gave his life!" Defiantly, she wiped her nose on the sleeve of her cotton garment. "*Now*, will you please, please find me something to wear besides this floursack? I think Dugan took my things out into the other room somewhere. *Please?*"

It was the first I'd heard of her having had a husband, that I could remember; but her marital status, or ex-marital status, could wait. She was right, of course. With two dead men on the premises who might be discovered at any moment, we didn't have too much time to waste.

"Sure," I said. "Don't go away, I'll be right back."

Out in the little attendants' room between the two prison suites of Goldenrod Cottage, I found a closet containing the pink slacks-shirt-and-sweater outfit she'd been wearing when I'd last seen her, including shoes and some flimsy underneath stuff I hadn't had the privilege of viewing previously although I could recall making an effort in that direction, unsuccessful. When I returned, she wasn't where I'd left her. I heard the shower running in the bathroom. Well, if she could worry about soap and water, I didn't have to worry about her. I went in there to find her just stepping out of the shower. Under other circumstances I might have been intrigued by the picture she made, reaching for a towel, but this wasn't the time or place. At the moment I didn't give a damn whether she was entrancingly nude like September Morn or armorplated like Joan of Arc; and apparently neither did she.

"What cause?" I asked.

"What?"

"Your husband gave his life for a great cause, you said."

Having given herself a quick rubdown, she started drying her hair. "The PPP, of course," she said a bit irritably. "The People's Protest Party. How corny can you get?"

It took me a moment to make the connection, even though I recalled now that I'd had some earlier suspicions that there was a connection.

I said, "Oh, you mean this terrorist outfit that goes around blowing things up? Like ferries." Busy with her hair, she only nodded. I summarized what I'd learned so far: "What you're saying is that your husband was a member of this outfit, he got killed, and now you've infiltrated it, is that the idea?"

"Yes, of course. They killed Roger, didn't they? Oh, they tried to make me think he blew himself up accidentally while doing their horrible work with Dan Market, and of course I pretended to believe them so they'd trust me, but actually Roger was sick of the whole terrible business. He was planning to . . . to blow the whistle on them as you Yankees say. Obviously they planned his death to silence him. So I tried to get some evidence by . . . by getting involved with them myself." She tossed aside the towel, found a comb on the glass shelf above the washbowl, and started working with it painfully. "That was back east where Roger was killed. Toronto. Then they had me move out here to the West Coast and run a few unimportant errands for them. I knew that they were just testing my loyalty, and that they didn't really trust me and probably never would. I realized I was getting in over my head so I secretly got in touch with one of the investigators who'd questioned me after the Toronto explosion—an RCMP man named Ross; you saw him at the hospital—and asked for help and protection."

"Me?"

"As it turned out, they sent me you. Of course we had to get acquainted very elaborately and sneakily so as not to arouse suspicion. . . ." She threw the comb aside. "I don't know why I'm worrying about my bloody *hair!*

69

Where did you put my. . . . Oh, thanks!" She giggled abruptly. "You make a wonderful ladies' maid, Mr. Madden. Have you had a great deal of experience?"

"Unfortunately, I don't remember," I said. "It seems to me I could have been told some of this stuff before now."

"In that hospital room? It was . . . there was a microphone in it. And on the telephone, too. Bugged, is that the word?"

"Bugged," I said. "But the plane we took to Vancouver wasn't bugged, was it?"

She said, a bit uncomfortably, "Well, that man in Washington, Mac, felt that since we were going to turn you over to them, the less you knew the better."

"Sure, my pal, Mac." I grimaced. "Where does the Chinese girl, Sally Wong, come into all this?"

"You'd been working with her on another aspect of the case that had led nowhere, I understand. They took you off that and assigned you to me."

So the oriental menace wasn't. Well, you can't be right all the time. Kitty was buttoning her shirt. I passed the pants over and she stepped into them.

"All that business about your doing a story on the lumber business," she said, zipping herself up, "and ditching the pretty airlines girl because you'd fallen for the lovely PR lady at first sight. . . . Rather trite, but it seemed to work. I was questioned about you, of course but Joan Market seemed to accept my answers. But if I'd refused to bring you here when she ordered me to last week, she'd have known I was lying when I now claimed to hate you violently because you'd just been revealed as a sneaky U.S. agent trying to destroy the PPP, who'd wormed his way into my affections pretending to be a harmless photographer." In spite of her damp and tangled hair and hastily assembled costume, there was a hint of the old Kitty about her as she grinned at me maliciously. "Hi, worm."

She was making a fast comeback, but it was hardly the ideal spot for flirtation. It wasn't even a very good spot for interrogation; but there was no way of knowing what would happen next, and I preferred not to operate in the dark when the knowledge was available.

"What's a Market?" I asked. "Who's Joan? Who's Dan?"

"Where are my shoes? Just set them down there, thanks. . . ." She held my arm for balance, stepping into them. She said, "Joan Market is my contact, I guess you'd call her; the person through whom I infiltrated the PPP. Rather a hippie type, fuzzy hairdo, long denim skirt, and very suspicious; but it wasn't too difficult to convince her I wanted to pick up the flaming torch of freedom where my martyred husband had dropped it—and if you think that's corny, you should hear them talk some time—since her husband, Dan, had been killed with Roger in that Toronto blast." Kitty was struggling into her pink sweater and pulling her long hair out from under it. "Now can we go?"

"What went wrong? How did you wind up here?"

She said impatiently, "Well, naturally they'd been suspicious of me—even more suspicious of me—since they learned who you really were. I don't know how your chief or whoever he is came to make that slip, using your real name over the phone so they could trace you. I'd told him from the start they were listening to everything that was said in that room and over that telephone. After . . . after using me to get you here, I guess they decided I wasn't much good to them any more and they'd find out exactly where I did stand." She hesitated. "I . . . I told them, Paul, I told them everything."

I grinned. "Hell, so did I. Everything I knew, at least. Who wants to be a hero? But what they really wanted to know I couldn't remember. Walters, Walters, Walters. What's so damned important about Herbert Walters, anyway?"

"Isn't that obvious? He was one of them; at least he sat in on the meetings of the council. He knows—knew —all about their next operation."

I thought that over for a minute and whistled softly. "Now it begins to add up! They've got another big bang all set to go, is that it? But if the missing Walters compromised their plans they're going to have to abort. . . . Sure. They've got to know if it's safe to go ahead.

71

I don't suppose you know what they're preparing to blow up next?"

She shook her head quickly. "Heavens, no! That's very high-echelon business. I was just a raw recruit on probation. . . . *Please*, Paul. Can't we leave now? This place gives me the horrors."

I nodded. "That's it with the questions. Ready for Operation Breakout. Firearms first. What happened to the gun you had?"

"They took it back, of course—it was theirs to start with—but I've no idea where it went to."

"Well, we could spend all night looking for a gun cabinet," I said. "To hell with it. I'll get one off a guard. There's not much chance of surprising the inside security man, the one on the front door, not with a lot of ambulatory patients and their attendants lounging around the lobby after dinner. However, the outside man makes his first evening round at dinner time, and if he's on schedule he ought to be coming back towards Aster shortly. There's a lovely bunch of dripping lilac bushes for me to hide in right at the corner of the cottage. . . . Remember, when I tell you to stay some place and don't move, you stay there and don't move, no matter how deep you sink in the mud or how hard it rains on you."

Kitty was looking a little pale. "I'll do my best, Paul."

Actually, it was easy. It was drizzling fairly heavily by now, and the security guard, a thickset middleaged man, was wrapped in a long black rubbery raincoat that gleamed wetly under the hazy lights. It rustled so loudly as he walked that he couldn't have heard the roar of a charging lion, and it didn't help his maneuverability a bit when I jumped him from behind. The first blow from Dugan's cosh knocked off his uniform cap and sent him to hands and knees.

I picked my spot carefully, and struck a second time, harder. He was dead before he subsided on the wet bricks of the walk.

ELEVEN

It didn't take me long to become the possessor of a .38 Colt revolver with a six-inch barrel, a fairly husky weapon designed for holster use. A little further searching gave me a trick rubber cartridge holder, a quick-load device with six extra rounds all lined up ready to be slapped in the cylinder—I wondered what kind of a fire-fight he'd been anticipating on these medical premises. I also acquired a wallet and some more keys. I hoped I wouldn't have to do any swimming before the night was over. The amount of metal I was now carrying, I'd sink like a stone.

I turned my head and whistled softly. A light figure detached itself from the wet bushes and came splashing towards me across the soggy lawn. Pale pink wasn't, I reflected, a very practical color for this type of night-escape operation. The next time we had to blast out of a booby hatch together, I hoped she'd pick a more suitable color scheme, not to mention a pair of pants she could run in without tripping over the super-stylish, super-wide cuffs—even as I watched, she got her feet tangled and fell headlong. Not that it mattered. By this time we were both about as wet and muddy as we could get. I stepped forward and helped her up.

"Grab the feet," I hissed, leading her back to the corpus delecti. "The old goat is too heavy for me to carry and I don't want to direct attention to him by leaving a plowed-up trail where I dragged him across the lawn. . . . What's the matter?"

"But . . . but this man is *dead!*" There was horror in her voice. "You *killed* him."

I drew a long breath, and told myself firmly that I was a reasonable person, not given to violent displays of temper.

"Miss Davidson," I said calmly, "you're quite welcome to try to get out of here by yourself. I tell you what, ma'am, although it involves some risk I'll give you half an hour to do it your way. I'll wait right here. After that I'll go out of here my way. That should keep us both happy, right?" I looked at her standing there in the soaking rain. "Well, what the hell are you waiting for? You don't seem to like my escape technique so go ahead and use your own."

She was looking down at the man on the walk between us. Her wet face was white and strained. "But you didn't *have* to—"

"Don't tell me what I do or don't have to do!" I snapped, to hell with being reasonable. "I don't owe these crummy bastards anything, not one thing except a week of hell! I'm not obliged to take a single goddamned risk to keep them healthy; as far as I'm concerned it's open season at Inanook and no bag limit. I gave them a clear warning the day you brought me here. They chose to ignore it. Now I'm leaving, and anybody who gets in my way is dead!"

"But he didn't get in your way! He was just—"

"Just strolling around the property with a loaded gun!" I sneered. "A gun he could have shot us with if something went wrong. Even if I hadn't wanted the pistol for myself, I'd have put him out of action so he couldn't use it. You don't leave armed characters wandering around behind you if you can help it." This was idiotic, having to explain basic principles with the rain pouring down and the clock ticking. "It's your decision, doll, but make it fast. Either give me a hand with the dirty work, or see how far you get being gentle and humanitarian by yourself."

She hesitated a moment longer, staring up at me. "Dugan?" she whispered. "How did you know we didn't have to worry about Dugan? Did you kill him, too?"

"Are you going to cry for *Dugan,* for God's sake?"

She was regarding me strangely. "And the one in your cottage, the big blond boy they call Tommy? I don't suppose he stepped aside politely and let you walk out."

"I feel kind of bad about Tommy," I said. "He wasn't really a bad guy."

Surpisingly, she made a choked little sound that turned out to be a giggle. Well, almost.

"You're really rather a monster, aren't you, darling. I hadn't realized."

It took me aback, a little. I guess I hadn't realized, either. When I came to think of it, I didn't know where those basic principles came from that I'd been explaining to her, any more than I could remember where I'd learned the blow that had killed Tommy Trask. I'd merely been acting in a manner that seemed necessary and natural; but I could see that by conventional, civilized standards my recent behavior might appear to be a little crude. We stood there in silence for a moment— silence, that is, except for the steady rustling of the rain. At last Kitty laughed oddly.

"I'm sorry. I think I'm being stupid. I'm supposed to be working for revenge on these people, aren't I? Why should I care how many of them die?" Deliberately, she squeezed the soaked hair back from her face so it wouldn't obscure her vision when she bent over. She swallowed hard, reached down, and grasped the ankles. "Well, where do you want it?"

Ten minutes later, after ducking around bungalows and crawling through occasional bushes to avoid raincoated employees hurrying between the cottages and the kitchen with trays of dirty dishes, we reached the main house. In the darkness at the side of the building it took me a while to locate the right key on Dugan's ring. My fingers were numb with cold and slippery with rain. I was beginning to think I was going to have to work my way through the guard's assortment to find the one I wanted, although I knew Dugan had carried one because I'd seen him use it; then a key finally turned in my clumsy grasp and the door opened.

Kitty whispered, "Do we have to go in *there?*" Before

75

I could answer, she said quickly, "Sorry again. It's just Davidson being stupid again."

In the treatment room, a small night light was burning. The place still stank of human suffering and its by-products. Kitty slipped around by way of the wall, keeping as far as possible from the equipment with which we'd both become too familiar. I forced myself to walk straight across the tiled floor, and pat the table and chair lightly as I went by, just to show them they didn't scare me a bit. I don't think I fooled them much, or myself, either. It was never going to be my favorite place.

I opened the inner door very cautiously, gun ready. Another small light burned in Dr. Elsie's examining room. Her office, beyond an open door, seemed to be fully lighted. I moved silently that way and peeked. She wasn't there. I signaled to Kitty to join me and went in. Somehow, the soft carpet and neat office furniture seemed to emphasize how wet we were, but I checked Kitty with a gesture when she instinctively embarked on a campaign of sartorial reconstruction. I pointed to the chair behind the desk.

"Just sit there and don't move," I said. "You're the bait. We're waiting for the tiger. I mean, tigress."

I stepped back into the corner by the soundproof door that led out into the lobby. The inside guard would be in his cubicle, I knew, and there would be inmates—Dr. Elsie referred to them as patients, but Dr. Albert preferred to call them guests—talking, reading, or just staring at the walls out there, but nothing could be heard in the well-insulated office, just as no screams from the back room could be heard in the lobby. I felt a belated rivulet of ice water trickle down my neck. Kitty had her elbows on the desk as she watched the door half-fearfully. Rain from her sweater and her long hair was soaking into the otherwise unmarked green blotter on the desk. Not too many executives went in for desk blotters these ballpoint days, I reflected, but Elsie was an old-fashioned girl.

I knew her pretty well by now. I knew she'd be back soon. Perhaps because she had such fun ways of using electricity, she hated to see it wasted. She wouldn't have left all the lights on in here if she wasn't returning to the office shortly. . . . Then the doorknob turned, and she marched in briskly, her starched coat rustling. She stopped short, staring at the girl who'd usurped the chair behind the desk. The moment of surprise was enough; the heavy door closed itself behind her, with a little encouragement from me, before she could throw herself backwards out of danger, or call for help.

"Careful, Doctor," I said. "There's a gun on you."

She didn't turn her head. She was really quite a woman, in her grotesque, middleaged way.

"Mr. Madden?"

"With a revolver in my hand, I think I'm Helm," I said. "Madden is the guy with the camera."

"It must be confusing," she said calmly. She turned, very slowly and carefully. There was a little pause. She didn't bother with the obvious questions like how did I get out and what the hell did I think I was doing and did I really think I could get away with it. She merely said, "Apparently I underestimated you. We get so many blustering loudmouths who are going to tear this place down brick by brick if we don't release them immediately with abject apologies. Are you going to kill me now?"

I said, "It would be fun, but I'll pass as long as you behave yourself," I said. "I don't really need to do it for personal satisfaction. I killed you every day in that back room. Little by little, piece by piece."

Her hoarse voice said, "Of course. They all do."

"Actually, it wouldn't be so good if you were really dead," I said. "The dead don't suffer. As long as you're alive I can hope that the remission of your disease, if that's the proper medical jargon, is only temporary. When it comes back it will do a slower and better job on you than I could ever do."

Her eyes narrowed under the thick brows. I saw that I'd hit home. It was something she feared, perhaps the only thing she feared. Her face looked like something out of a prehistoric nightmare, the kind that Pacific island savages used to commemorate with stone statues. She glanced bleakly at Kitty.

"All this because a stupid girl conceived an idiot revenge for the death of her wishy-washy husband!" she sneered. "You miserable intellectual midgets! Just because we dealt summarily with a weakling traitor, girl, do you think that gives you the right to deceive and betray us, too? And you, Helm, an establishment mercenary taking advantage of her sentimental grief to further the oppressive purposes of your ruthless government employers in the United States, and their accomplices here in Canada; all trying vainly to put down a great, spontaneous, revolutionary movement far more important to the future of mankind than a single life, or a hundred lives, or a thousand. . . . Kill him, Jake!"

It might have worked. She'd held my attention nicely with her gaudy talk of revolution; but the guard who walked in on us was very, very slow. He had a strap on his holster and I guess he'd never practiced unsnapping it in a hurry. When he opened the door casually, and saw us standing there, and heard Elsie's sharp command, he lunged forward clawing at his hip. I saw at once that he wasn't Wyatt Earp reincarnated, no matter what he might think. I took time to bring the heavy gun barrel down hard on Elsie's wrist as she grabbed for my weapon. I was still in no danger as I stepped into the clear and raised the Colt once more and took deliberate aim. . . .

Gradually, Jake realized that he was dead; the certificate just hadn't been signed yet to make it official. With his weapon half out of the holster, he froze.

"Wrong grip," I said. "Two fingers. Lay it gently on the desk, please."

TWELVE

Then everything and everybody stood quite still for a moment—well, Kitty remained seated behind the desk—while I took stock of the situation. The important thing to keep in mind, I told myself, was that the guard hadn't known he was walking into trouble, or he'd have had the revolver in his hand or, at least, had the retaining strap off. This indicated that Dr. Elsie hadn't managed to set off an alarm by means, say of a button hidden under the office carpet or a communicator in the pocket of her white coat. However, she had known he was coming. She'd been doing her best to distract me with conversation while she waited for him to arrive. Maybe that was why she'd left the lights on in here; she'd had an evening appointment with the guy, to give him a raise, fire him, bawl him out, or just hand him his weekly check.

No sounds reached us through the soundproof door. Nobody charged in to see what was wrong, or called us on the phone to say we were surrounded and had better come out quietly with our hands up. Apparently, Jake had not been seen reaching clumsily for his gun as he entered, before the spring-loaded door closed behind him; or if he had been seen, it was only by a disturbed patient with overriding problems of his own.

"I think it's broken," Elsie said, clutching the wrist I'd hammered with the gunbarrel.

"Swell," I said. "Nothing like a little good news on a dreary day. What do you expect, Doctor, sympathy? Now take off your coat, please. That may be just a stethoscope you're carrying in the pocket, but let me have the fun of finding it out for myself, huh? Oh, and please give me a running report on how much it hurts your poor smashed wrist. I do want to hear every agonizing detail."

I watched her slip out of the starched garment, favoring the injured arm, if it really was injured beyond a moderate bruise. Somehow I didn't have a great deal of faith in that fracture, nor did I intend to base any plans on her disabled condition.

I said, "Now drop it on the floor and take a seat in that conversation nook over there. You, too, Jake. What's your full name?"

He was a lean, pale-eyed, older man with bushy gray eyebrows, and a bushy gray moustache. He looked like the picturesque-old-plainsman type beloved by the movies and TV, the homespun character who chews tobacco and produces dry scraps of backwoods philosophy while he guides the intrepid hero to the hidden canyon where the trembling ingenue is being held captive by the renegade redskins. It was disillusioning to think that a guy with a fine frontier face like that didn't know how to draw a gun properly. He'd never make it as a Hollywood sheriff until he learned. Maybe that was why he was working as a uniformed guard in a place like this.

"Frechette," he said in a subdued, accented voice. "My name it is Jacques Frechette."

"Okay. Go take a seat, Mr. Frechette. You're less likely to get active ideas sitting down."

"Oui, Monsieur."

I watched him carefully as he moved to one of the three comfortably upholstered chairs—one had already been taken by Elsie—grouped around a low round table at the end of the big office, perhaps for informal doctor-patient consultations, perhaps for staff policy conferences on matters medical and otherwise. Three similar chairs stood back against the wall awaiting a real crowd. There was a phone on the table. There was also a phone on the desk. There was also a gun, now, on the desk.

"Kitty," I said, indicating Frechette's weapon, "can you use that? Not just wave it around like you did that

80

toy hideout pistol when you brought me here, but really use it?"

She shook her head quickly. "I'm sorry, Paul. I . . . actually I was brought up to think they were terrible. I've never really fired one."

I said sourly, "Someday somebody's going to have to explain to me what's so wonderful about raising a generation of helpless, gunless victims these times of crime and violence. Well, take it anyway, but try not to blow my head off."

I was still watching the office door warily, waiting for a rescue expedition to come crashing through it, but none did. At last I allowed myself to relax a little. I picked up Elsie's coat and found nothing in the pockets but the stethoscope I'd already spotted. I was tempted to ask her what a head doctor was doing with a chest-listening device, but maybe it was a status badge like the binoculars worn by the Officer of the Deck on a Navy ship, even in port. I hung the garment on an old-fashioned tree-like stand in the corner. I closed the door on the examining room with its scalpels and acids that might serve as impromptu weapons in a pinch. I went back and relieved some of the load on my belt by digging out the three wallets distorting my pockets, and the three bunches of keys, all of which I dumped on the desk blotter. I pointed to the wallets.

"Just to bring you up to date, Mr. Frechette," I said, "the former owners of those wallets did not contribute voluntarily to the Helm going-away fund. I'd hate to have to add your wallet to the collection, but I wouldn't hate it very much, so I hope you'll see your way clear to cooperating with me."

The security man licked his lips. "In what way, Monsieur?"

"Can you summon Dr. Caine without arousing his suspicions? Don't say yes if you can't produce."

Frechette looked puzzled. "You want me to ask the Director to come here?"

"That's right."

"It would sound more natural if Dr. Somerset called him, sir."

"I know that," I said. "But Dr. Somerset would happily allow me to shoot her to death if she could just manage to gasp out a warning first. I'm hoping you're not quite so ready to die, Mr. Frechette."

The uniformed man frowned as if he found thinking painful, then he brightened. "I could tell Dr. Caine that Dr. Somerset had asked me to make the call for her, sir."

"Do it," I said.

"I . . . I think Dr. Caine will still be in the dining room."

He was. We waited for him to come to the phone. I listened in on the desk extension. It seemed to go all right. If any code words were passed, signaling emergency, I didn't spot them. Waiting, afterwards, I tried to kid myself that my clothes were actually drying and I was getting a little warmer. I was aware of Kitty shivering uncontrollably from time to time. Abruptly, the door opened.

"What's so urgent it couldn't wait fifteen minutes—"

Dr. Caine stopped abruptly. The door sighed closed behind him. His glance shifted from me to Kitty to the seated pair by the round table, and back to me and the gun I held.

"What's going on here?" he blustered. "I must warn you, Madden, that we've had plenty of practice in dealing with violent patients attempting to escape from this institution. You have no chance whatever to get away, so please put down that weapon and be sensible. It will be all the worse for you if you hurt somebody."

I regarded him for a moment. Apparently he didn't wear his doctor-coat to dinner; he was very distinguished-looking in a dark suit with a neat white stripe. He looked as if he'd have a great bedside manner, but I didn't judge he'd take a lot of pressure, which was why I'd got him here.

I said, "That's very unfortunate, because Trask is lying in Hyacinth with a broken neck. Dugan is lying outside Goldenrod with a broken neck. Your outside guard, who was so kind as to contribute this gun, is lying outside Aster with a fractured skull. Dr. Somerset claims to have a fractured wrist. So I'm afraid I've already hurt some people, Albert. I guess I'll just have to take my medicine, whatever it is."

"My God!" he whispered. "My God, you must be mad!"

"Well, you'd be just the man to know about it, director of a place like this, wouldn't you?" I said. I straightened up from the desk on which I'd been half-sitting. "Now it's your turn. I don't figure it's much use my trying to interrogate Dr. Elsie over there, much as I'd love it. She looks pretty tough to me. You look more like a person'd listen to reason. Anyway, if I work on you, I've got help available."

He swallowed. "Interrogate? I can't imagine what you think I could tell you—"

I said, "I want to know the identity of the Observer."

"Who?"

I said, "I mean the small, corpulent character who stood in the corner and watched all the fun back there in Elsie's recreation room. Don't claim you never saw him, Albert, because I remember a couple of times when you stuck your head in the door and he was there."

Dr. Caine's handsome face was pale. He licked his lips. "I'm sorry, I really don't know who that man—" He stopped, hearing the sharp click of the revolver coming to full cock. "Oh, *that* man!" he said breathlessly. "Yes, yes, of course, but I'm afraid I can't tell you. . . . I mean, he just comes and goes as he pleases, Mr. Madden. Lewis brings him in the Mercedes, that's all I know. I don't know his name, really. I haven't . . . haven't been permitted to know it." He glanced resentfully towards Elsie. "They . . . they don't take me into their confidence, Mr. Madden; they keep me completely in the dark, I swear it. They just force me to allow these premises to be used . . . an unfortunate incident in my past, totally misunderstood. It's sheer blackmail, Mr. Madden."

"I want the little man's name," I said when he finally ran down.

"I swear I don't know it! I swear it!"

I said, "That's too bad, Albert. That's really too bad. Okay, let's go." I gestured with the gun.

"What . . . what are you going to do?"

I asked irritably, "What the hell do you think I'm going to do? I've got the electrical equipment, and I know from personal experience that it's very effective. I've got the lady expert to run it—I told you I had help available. We'll determine scientifically just what you know and what you don't."

"You mean . . . you're going to take me back *there?*"

"I've been there. Kitty's been there. What's so damned special about you?" I grimaced. "Elsie's feeling deprived. All her pretty human toys have been taken away. She's got nobody left to play with. We wouldn't want her getting totally frustrated, would we? We'll start in the chair, I think. I doubt that you're stubborn enough to require the special attentions for which she uses the table. It's too bad you've just had your dinner, of course. It means that you'll undoubtedly spew all over yourself when she hits the button. Then, since you haven't been properly prepared the way Kitty and I were, you'll probably shit your pants full; but by that time you'll be having such wonderful electrical convulsions you won't even care."

"But you *can't!*" he gasped

"It will be the greatest pleasure I've had in months, Albert, more fun even than wringing Dugan's neck," I said cheerfully. "I'm really looking forward to it. However, there's an unfortunate possibility that my enjoyment won't last very long."

He licked his lips. "What . . . what do you mean?"

"Well," I said deliberately, "I don't know how to run that shock machine. Only Elsie knows; and she seems to take this mystery crusade of hers, or revolution, or whatever it is, very seriously. She told me herself it was much more important than a mere human life, or even a thousand mere human lives. If you have information that threatens it, she won't want you telling me, will she? That means there's a good chance that, being a logical lady, after we've got you strapped in the chair with all electrodes properly attached, she'll simply rev up her volts and fry you permanently before you can talk. . . . Well, you know her better than I do. Maybe she'd never dream of treating a colleague in such an unfriendly way.

And of course if you really don't know anything, as you claim, you're perfectly safe."

Dr. Caine licked his pale lips and glanced at the ugly, craggy face of the woman seated at the end of the room.

"Ovid," he whispered. "The name is John Ovid. . . ."

THIRTEEN

It took Kitty a little while to figure out how to get an outside line; after that, Washington, D.C., U.S.A., was easy. She shoved the phone base across the desk and offered me the handset. I put it to my ear lefthanded. There was a certain amount of suspense as I listened to the ringing at the far end. In a sense I was calling my own past, long distance.

When the voice came on, I recognized it at once. It was the voice that had called me at the hospital and introduced me to the name Helm.

"Yes?"

"I'm calling from the Inanook Sanitarium somewhere near Vancouver, B.C.," I said carefully. "I think I want to talk with somebody called Mac."

"I'm Mac," the voice said. "At least I'm so called by some people under certain circumstances. Greetings, Eric."

"Who's Eric?" I asked.

"You are, in our records, filed under the agent's code name. . . . I gather your memory has not returned."

"I'm accumulating lots of information but few recollections," I said. "I'm told I work for you. Tell me something about how we operate, sir. Do we have research facilities? Internment facilities? Useful contacts with the Canadian authorities?"

"All are available within limits," said the man called Mac, three thousand miles away. "What do you require?"

"Reinforcements, first," I said. "But the reinforcements

should be properly briefed, sir, because some discreet burials will be required—"

"Just a minute!" There was suspicion in Mac's sharp voice. "Are you quite sure you remember nothing of our former relationship?"

"Nothing comes back, sir. I wouldn't recognize you if I met you on the street. Why?"

"Because you are the only operative who habitually addresses me in that overly respectful way. It is an old joke, or custom, between us."

I thought that over for a moment, and said, "Maybe my tongue remembers more than my brain, sir. Or maybe I'm just naturally smart enough to know that I'm more apt to get the help I need if I ask for it respectfully."

"To be sure. How many bodies?"

"Three so far, but the evening's young yet."

I looked meaningfully towards Dr. Elsie, who'd started to lean towards the uniformed guard beside her, perhaps to whisper some escape instructions. She saw me looking and straightened up in her chair. The guard seemed not to have noticed; and Dr. Albert sat stiffly in his chair looking as if the other two were total strangers whose acquaintance he had no desire to make.

Mac said, "Very well. Go on."

"A little official manpower is indicated," I said. "I've got the inner citadel secured, so to speak, but the rest of the fortress is still in enemy hands. I also have some of the staff under my gun, but I don't know how many of the others are involved with this Threepee outfit; and even perfectly innocent employees may misunderstand the situation and get very hostile. I'm pretty well armed and I can probably shoot my way clear if I have to, but I hate to see the butcher bill get much bigger. I'm hoping you can send somebody with a badge to pry me loose; somebody who knows the score. Tell him to come straight to the assistant director's office off the main lobby. What's a good code knock?"

"We use three and two as a rule."

"Okay, but they'd better use a gunbutt. It's a soundproof door. I'll hang on while you get them moving."

There was a period of silence. Kitty shifted position

uncomfortably, as if her damp clothes were sticking to the chair, or to her. I didn't look at her. I kept my attention where it belonged, on the woman who was the only real source of danger here, but Elsie didn't move and nobody else stirred. It occurred to me that I was calling three thousand miles across a continent to have Mac call three thousand miles back to speak to some officials who were probably located practically around the corner from me.

His voice returned. "So. They estimate twenty minutes."

"Good enough," I said. It was strange to be talking so easily with this man I couldn't remember at all; and I said a bit more stiffly, "I hope the experiment turned out in a satisfactory manner, sir."

There was another silence. "What experiment?"

"Arranging for an agent who'd lost his memory to be thrown to the sharks, just hoping he'd remember how to bite back."

I heard Mac laugh shortly at the other end of the line. "So far I would call the experiment a success. After all, you're alive, you've found the place for which we've been searching—one of the places; we have reason to believe the PPP has at least one more hidden refuge in the area—and you seem to have the upper hand. Let me point out that I did my best to protect you by revealing your true name. There are individuals involved who, while they would wipe out an annoying photographer ruthlessly, would hesitate a long time before doing permanent harm to one of our people. We try to demonstrate, from time to time, that it is a very expensive proposition."

I remembered the little man in the corner of the torture chamber, and the way he'd kept Dr. Elsie in line, and the reasons he'd given.

"Yes, sir," I said. "The message got through, which is why I'm still here with my brains more or less intact."

"Furthermore," he went on, "I not only had satisfactory reports from the medical staff of the hospital, but the agent with whom you'd been associated earlier, although she does not operate under my authority, was kind enough to pay you a visit and give me her opinion, reassuring as it turned out, on your condition."

I said, "So that's why she popped in that day. Whose authority does she operate under if not yours?"

"Since I gather you're not speaking from a safe phone, I'd better not tell you that. However, you should know that there were two separate and independent investigations, one of which, the one with which you and Miss Wong were concerned, seemed at first to have nothing to do with bombs or terrorists. Miss Wong discovered that there actually was no separation when she witnessed a meeting between her subject, Herbert Walters, and a subject connected with the other investigation, a certain Joan Market."

"I've been told about Mrs. Market," I said. "So I was switched over from Mission X to Mission Y, or vice versa?"

"Yes, the anti-terrorist operation had priority over Miss Wong's mission, although you still maintained contact with the lady and rendered her assistance to the extent permitted by your new duties." Mac paused. "But we haven't got time to go into the details now. You wanted some research done."

"That's right," I said. "First, John Ovid. Ovid, like the Roman poet, or was he Greek."

"Roman, I believe."

I said, "Height about five-two, weight around one-seventy, a real little butterball. German accent. Address unknown, but transportation is provided for him by a sanitarium limousine driven by a guy named Lewis. Wait a minute, I heard the first name once: Gavin Lewis. If they grab Lewis maybe they can get a lead to Ovid. He seems to be in touch with the PPP council, as they call it; he wields considerable authority. And then there's Dr. Albert Caine, and there's Dr. Elsie Somerset, director and assistant director of this bughouse—"

I saw Albert wince. Even under these strained circumstances, he obviously felt I should be referring to his institution with more respect. Elsie was staring into space, drumming her fingers on the round conference table in an absent way.

I said, sharply: "Keep them still or I'll shoot them off."

She glanced at me calmly, but her fingers stopped

moving. Mac spoke in my ear: "Eric?"

"Sorry, sir. A minor matter of discipline."

"I just had a preliminary report on the Inanook Sanitarium placed on my desk," he said. "It largely concerns the director you just asked about, Dr. Caine. He was a highly respected New York psychiatrist; however he was caught *in flagrante delicto*, as the old saying goes, with a female patient. Apparently he wound up as head of this obscure sanitarium after fleeing the scandal that cost him his lucrative practice in the East."

I said, "Hell, there's got to be more to it than that. I thought it was practically taken for granted, nowadays, that handsome male psychiatrists, society division, sleep with their female patients as part of the treatment."

Albert looked as if he wanted to protest this slander against his profession. Elsie continued to stare at the wall. I didn't like her frozen expression. Instinct told me that, behind it, she was planning her move; it was just a matter of time now. The old-plainsman type beside her seemed to have withdrawn into his shell also. He could have been asleep, but I didn't think he was.

Mac said, "You're quite right. Dr. Caine's problem was that he picked the wrong woman. She happened to be married to one Emilio Brassaro, a syndicate-affiliated gentleman with, among other illicit enterprises, a thriving import business involving Central and South America. You can guess the nature of the imports. Apparently, Mr. Brassaro does not qualify as a complaisant husband. Dr. Caine fled from New York in fear of his life, and Mrs. Brassaro required fairly extensive plastic surgery—apparently she was beaten quite badly, although it was reported as an automobile accident. You will be interested to hear that the person who actually inflicted the 'accident' upon Mrs. Grace Brassaro, we have learned, was Mr. Brassaro's right hand man, a certain Walter Christofferson. You know him—or knew him, depending on his current status—as Herbert Walters."

I said, "Let me get this straight. Walters, the guy who piloted the plane in which I crashed up in Hecate Strait, was actually a hood in the employ of a New York syndicate bigshot? Is that supposed to make sense—"

That was when the lady doctor went into action. She and Frechette moved simultaneously, heaving the low round table up on edge so that for a moment I couldn't see which way anybody was going behind it. Then the uniformed man emerged, heading for the lobby door. I fired. Plaster sprayed from the wall in front of Frechette, where I'd aimed. He came to an abrupt halt, his hands rising. The upturned table, after teetering on edge for a moment, crashed clear over, legs in the air. I caught a glimpse of Elsie struggling with the door to the examining room; she'd deliberately used the guard as a decoy to draw my attention the other way.

Before I could change my aim, before Elsie could get the door open, her body jerked strangely. I heard the crash of a firearm that wasn't mine. Instinctively, not quite comprehending what was happening, I threw myself aside and down. I heard another shot, and another. . . .

Looking up, I saw Kitty standing behind the desk with Frechette's big revolver clutched in both hands and tears streaming down her face as she hauled back the trigger repeatedly until the firing pin struck a discharged cartridge with a small, snapping noise that was ridiculously feeble after the shattering sounds that had preceded it. The office stopped shaking with the crash of gunfire. I glanced around. Frechette was gone; he'd taken advantage of the violent disturbance to slip away. Dr. Albert was on the floor where he'd thrown himself. He was whimpering fearfully but apparently unhurt.

Elsie lay by the inner door. I rose and went over to her. There was blood on the side of her face; and her dark sweater showed darker stains that glistened wetly. Her eyes opened and found me.

"It *was* broken," she whispered, and died.

I looked down at the ugly, diseased features and at the swollen wrist that had betrayed her when, forgetting, she'd tried to turn the knob with that hand. I don't know why I had an impulse to apologize, but I did. It was several seconds before I rose and went to Kitty, still standing there, and took the empty revolver from her hand and reloaded it from the spare-cartridge gadget I'd got from the outside guard. It was an interesting little device that I'd never used before, that I could remember. Then I went over to the dangling telephone, explained what had happened, and hung up. We waited without speaking because there didn't seem to be much to say.

Presently somebody knocked on the door three times with a heavy object. Two thumps followed. The armed man who entered cautiously—well, the first one in; there were plenty more behind him—was the chunky, dark-faced gent in civilian clothes who was supposed to have some connection with the Royal Canadian Mounted Police, the silent one who'd attended my plane-crash interrogation in Prince Rupert. I remembered that Kitty had told me his name quite recently: Ross. He said for me to hand over my weapons and everything would be just fine.

It seemed like a hell of a big promise for anybody, even a Mountie, to make.

FOURTEEN

It was still raining as we drove across a wide, modern freeway-type bridge over water and, disregarding numerous exit signs, took the divided highway up the long hill beyond. At the top of the hill, the big road swung left, westward. I had the feeling there were mountains above us, but in the dark and rain I had no real evidence of this.

"Am I supposed to know where I am?" I asked.

"You've been here plenty of times, darling," Kitty said. She was sitting beside me in the rear seat of the car. Our driver was the chunky brown gent who'd led the Inanook Relief Expedition. Kitty went on: "This is North Vancouver, where I live. Farther ahead on this road is West Vancouver. Back there across the water is Vancouver proper. Don't ever ask what happened to East and South Vancouver. Nobody knows and you'll just embarrass them by asking. The bridge we just crossed is called the Second Narrows Bridge because it bridges—guess what?—the Second Narrows of Burrard Inlet. There's also a First Narrows Bridge, also known as the Lions Gate Bridge. Does this sound familiar?"

"Well," I said, "it doesn't come as a tremendous surprise—I seem to have heard it before—but I couldn't have passed a test on the subject."

Kitty raised her voice slightly. "Take the next exit, please."

Our driver inclined his head to indicate that he'd heard. The official car—well, I thought it was an official car, although it had no markings—swung off the freeway, ducked beneath it by means of an underpass, and entered a maze of hilly little streets below, with individual houses bearing no resemblance to each other set back on reasonable-sized lots. It was the kind of oldfashioned suburb that existed before bulldozers and developments and identical split-level ranch houses were invented. There were trees and lawns. I made no effort to look for familiar landmarks. It had been a long night. I could work on improving my memory some other time.

We stopped in front of a white, two-story, frame house, still within sight and hearing of the freeway. I got out, since it seemed to be expected of me, and helped Kitty out.

"Thank you, Mr. Ross," she said politely to the driver. Her voice was perfect, but she seemed to be quite unaware, standing there in the rain, that she was rapidly getting soaked again after having pretty well dried off. "It was very nice of you to give us a lift, Mike," she said.

I was worried about her. She'd been totally calm and self-possessed about everything. Yes, she had shot Dr. Somerset. No, she didn't know very much about guns, but Paul had been busy dealing with the guard and she, Kitty, hadn't thought he wanted to let the woman get away. Yes, she was quite all right, thank you. No, she felt no need for a tranquilizer or sedative, thank you very much.

Now, for God's sake, she was lecturing me on local geography and graciously thanking our chauffeur for his trouble, like a normal young lady who hadn't just endured a lengthy imprisonment including a couple of days of ingenious torture, and hadn't just put three bullets out of six into a human target at six paces. Well, that was about average shooting for a beginner under stress, I seemed to recall, at that range, but the rest of her reactions weren't average at all. Either she was an iron-nerved maiden I'd misjudged completely, or she was grimly forcing herself to go through the civilized motions and keeping everything under control with a tremendous effort, probably the latter. Having enough mental problems of my own, I didn't particularly want to be present when hers surfaced and the strict control let go, but I had a hunch I would be.

"That's quite all right, Miss Davidson," the driver said. I had a feeling he might have called her Kitty if I hadn't been there. I gathered that we'd all got to know each other fairly well, working together earlier But my loss of memory, and the gory mess out at Inanook, had him treating us both with careful, impartial, policeman formality tonight. "Mr. Madden?" he said.

I closed the rear door of the car and moved up to the open front window. "Yes?"

"We still have a few matters to discuss. It's late now and you're tired. Where can I get in touch with you in the morning?"

Kitty took my arm possessively. "He'll be right here."

"Then, if I may, I'll come here. Around eleven?"

"That will be fine," she said. "I'll have some coffee for you."

We watched the car drive away, an ordinary, American-type, blue sedan. I was happy to see it go. I was a little tired of Canadian officialdom. Particularly, I was tired of Mr. Ross. Regardless of our previous association, he'd given me a tough time tonight. Apparently, in Canada, you weren't supposed to escape from insane asylums in which you were being illegally detained and semi-electrocuted. It got everybody all upset.

I reminded myself that, after all, I wasn't in jail. I didn't have handcuffs on. Maybe I was being ungrateful.

I turned to Kitty, who was fumbling in her purse—our smaller personal belongings had been found in the office safe, which Dr. Albert had been persuaded to open. We'd been told that, if our coats and bags were ever located, they'd be delivered to us. On the whole, I had to admit, we'd been treated with reasonable politeness, but there had been a strong aura of disapproval, strong enough that it hadn't seemed advisable to ask any nosy questions about how Ross and his associates were planning to dispose of, or explain away, the four dead bodies with which Kitty and I had saddled them. . . .

"It's the attic apartment," Kitty said, passing me a leather key-case with one key separated from the rest. "Don't you remember? The stairs are at the side of the house, over there. I'm sorry, I shouldn't twit you about your memory, should I?"

"Twit away," I said. "It doesn't hurt my feelings a bit."

We followed the wet walk to the side of the house and climbed the outside stairs in the steady rain. If I ever got out of this, I reflected, I'd find myself a nice tropical island with balmy breezes playing under cobalt-blue skies. I unlocked and opened the door and let Kitty pass me. She turned on the light, revealing a small modern kitchen mostly finished in natural wood.

"I think we need a drink, don't you?" she said. "Everything's over there to the right of the stove, except you'll find ice in the fridge. It's a little chilly, don't you think? Why don't I light the fire while you mix the drinks? I do think a fire would be nice, don't you? It's such a raw night out."

Her pleasant hostess manner was in sharp contrast with her rained-on and generally beat-up appearance, and the odd, unsmiling look in her eyes.

"Very nice," I said.

"It's Scotch with just one ice cube, darling. No water. And you're a martini man in case you forget. Oh, dear, I do keep referring to your poor memory, don't I?"

When I brought the drinks into the living room, which included a small dining nook by the window to the right, she was kneeling to stare into the fire. It was well alight; it must have been already laid. The fireplace, with a deep shaggy rug in front of it, was a brick installation in the end of the low, slant-ceilinged room. There was a door beside it that presumably led to a bedroom and bath beyond.

"Here you are," I said, reaching over her shoulder to put a glass into her hand.

She took it and sipped from it. She spoke without looking around, in the bright and cheerful voice she'd been using: "Those pressed sawdust logs aren't so romantic, but they're much easier to find nowadays, and it's nice to know that the sawdust from all our lumbermills is being put to some use, isn't it? They used to simply dump it, waste it." She took a deep drink from

96

her glass, and another, and polished off the contents with a final gulp, and handed it back to me. "Kitty wants more," she said in a phony-childish voice. "Kitty wants to get sozzled. Kitty is a murderess."

"It's your liquor," I said, and went back to the kitchen for refills, draining my own martini glass on the way. Whatever she had in mind, it didn't seem advisable to let her get too far ahead of me; and now that we were out of that place, the idea of getting sozzled, as she'd called it, had a definite attraction. There were things that had happened that could, I felt, be studied better through a rosy haze of alcohol. When I returned, she hadn't moved. I placed the glass into her hand as before. "Go a bit easy on that one, doll," I said. "It's loaded."

"I hope you're not planning to stay sober, darling." She was still kneeling there staring straight into the fire. "I need company. Sozzled company."

"I'm right with you," I said. "What are we celebrating, besides Liberation Day."

"I told you," she said. "I'm a murderess."

"Swell," I said. "Join the club."

There was a little pause while she struggled to her feet and turned at last to face me, already displaying some unsteadiness. I remembered that she'd been given no substantial food for quite a while. I remembered also that, a few beers excepted, I'd had no liquor at all within the extent of my limited recent memory. I could feel the unaccustomed alcohol taking effect. It promised to be an interesting, inebriated evening, what was left of it; but after what we'd both been through we had it coming. I couldn't see a single good reason for staying sober. Kitty took a deliberate, deep swig of her fresh drink, and looked at me gravely.

"No, you don't understand, Paul," she said, speaking carefully and clearly. "You don't understand at all. I didn't shoot that woman just to keep her from getting away, as I told everybody. I lied. I did it because I *wanted* to do it."

"Sure."

"But you don't *understand!*" she protested. "It was all that kept me alive in that dreadful room, knowing that some day, somehow, I'd have the pleasure of killing that sadistic bitch."

I said, "So what else is new?"

She frowned. "You, too?"

"Me, and probably everybody else who ever wore those straps and electrodes, at least for non-medical reasons. She said as much, remember?"

Kitty shook her head quickly. "It just seems so *incredible*. I've been prattling bravely about revenge but I never dreamed I'd *really*. . . . I was only thinking in terms of getting evidence so the law could. . . . I never suspected I was capable of. . . ." She giggled abruptly. "I seem to be quite incoherent, don't I?"

"I'm with you every step of the way," I said. "To incoherence, long may it wave."

We drank to that, and she said, "I was dreadfully shocked when you killed that guard, but now. . . . Really, all I feel is relieved, Paul. I suppose that's dreadful, but nobody should be allowed to do such degrading things to other people and survive. Now she's gone and I can breathe again. I don't have to think of her alive somewhere with that horrible face knowing things about me nobody ought to know. . . . Oh, my God!"

She was staring past me, wide-eyed. I turned, half-expecting attack, conscious that all the weapons I'd managed to commandeer with considerable effort had been taken from me, but nobody was there. Only the door of the coat closet was there, standing open to expose the full-length mirror inside that was designed to permit the lady of the house to make a last-minute hose-and-hairdo inspection before appearing in public.

I heard Kitty give a choked little giggle that was half a sob. She moved past me and posed in front of the glass to get the full effect: the stringy hair, the limp blouse collar above the snagged and sagging sweater, and the shapeless, voluminous pink slacks, ripped at one knee, smeared with the black loam of the landscaping through which we'd crawled, with the wide cuffs abjectly downtrodden and hopelessly filthy.

She began to laugh, staring at the apparition laughing

98

back at her. She raised her glass to the woebegone Kitty-caricature in the mirror, and finished off the contents. Then she swayed a little, choking on her laughter. I stepped forward to take the empty glass before she dropped it. Setting it aside with mine, also empty, I put my arm around her to steady her. She made an odd strangled sound in her throat, and turned with a shudder, and pressed her face against my shoulder.

"Easy," I said, "Take it easy, Kitty. It's all over now. You're all right now."

But the hysterics I was expecting didn't come. I felt her fight for control and win. She drew a deep, gasping breath and straightened up, running her grubby sweater-sleeve across her eyes.

"Good girl," I said. "Now you can duck into the bedroom and get out of those ridiculous pantaloons while I repair to the bar and replenish both our. . . . What's the matter?"

Her eyes were watching me in a speculative manner. Something had changed in the room. It had happened when I held her—when, about to let herself dissolve into helpless weeping and wild laughter, she'd clamped down the iron discipline once more. I decided that there was a great deal about this supposed fiancee of mine I didn't know. Suddenly she was no longer a poor weak girl on the edge of hysteria being comforted by a strong man after a terrible experience. Our roles had subtly been switched somehow, but I didn't know how.

She spoke deliberately: "If you want my ridiculous pantaloons removed, darling, why don't you do something about it?" There was a funny, hard edge to her voice. "You're the big Prince Rupert zipper expert, aren't you?"

I'll admit it shocked me. Not that I'd thought her sexless in spite of earlier misunderstandings, or that I would have totally rejected the idea, if it had been presented to me, that dainty Miss Davidson might even take the initiative under certain circumstances, but these weren't the circumstances. I would have bet on champagne and candlelight and filmy lingerie. Obviously, I'd have lost my bet. My slim and lovely lady, finding herself in an embarrassingly bedraggled condition, had apparently conceived a lowdown bedroom game that involved having me liberate her slender body from its cruel prison of grimy rags. . . .

"Well?" she demanded in that same hard voice. "What's the matter, Paul? Does your dream girl have to have a nice sharp crease in her pants before you'll condescend to undress—" She stopped abruptly. There was a moment of silence; then she drew a shaky breath and spoke in quite different tones, softly, almost pleadingly: "Please, darling. I make such an unconvincing nympho-maniac, don't I? Please help me. Don't you want to *know?*"

Something stirred uneasily in my mind. "Know what?"

"You're being stupid!" Some of the hardness returned to her voice. "You know perfectly well what I mean. You *must* understand!"

"Tell me," I said, but I knew I didn't really want to be told.

After a long moment, Kitty licked her lips and spoke carefully: "Well . . . well, she did some *weird* things to me, didn't she to you, darling? Didn't she? And don't you want to know if . . . if you're still a human being with all your reactions and impulses intact and not just a cheap electrical toy twitching obscenely on the end of a wire? And. . . ." She licked her lips once more. "And there's really only one way to find out, isn't there?"

There it was. She'd faced the thing I'd put aside. I'd shoved the nagging doubt far back into the dark recesses of my mind—there had, after all, been a few other things to worry about besides sex—and ordered my mind to forget it, something it seemed to be very good at these days. Now I had a sudden, clear, unwelcome memory of the steel table in the Torquemada room and the agonizing, electrical experiments performed by the woman with the stone face who'd made such a wonderful adjustment to her unfortunate disease.

"Okay," I breathed. "Okay. I dig you, doll. It's a little coldblooded, but okay."

We looked at each other for a moment—a rather embarrassed moment. Kitty laughed abruptly, looking down at herself.

"Of course, I'm not very sexy like this, am I? But

then you're not exactly God's gift to women right now. I think we can manage without perfume and aftershave lotion, don't you? If . . . if we can manage at all."

"What fornication-location did you have in mind, ma'am?"

"What about right here, darling? I always did have a secret ambition to get laid, as you Yankees so picturesquely put it, on a nice shaggy rug in front of an open fire. If you don't mind?"

"It sounds fine to me," I said judiciously. "Interesting. Beds are so commonplace, aren't they?"

"Paul."

"Yes?"

"This is rather ridiculous, isn't it? We're just standing here *talking*. Lift your arms, there's a good boy." When I obeyed, she grasped my turtleneck at the bottom and pulled it off over my head and tossed it aside. She put her arms up. "Your turn."

I stripped off and discarded her ruined sweater. Suddenly she was in my arms, turning her face up for the kiss. I felt as awkward and inexperienced as if I'd never held a woman before. I told myself that, as she herself had pointed out, she wasn't the most seductive figure in the world at the moment; but I knew I was just kidding myself. Actually, I found her kind of perversely appealing in her dirty-pink tramp outfit, if only because it was so obviously expendable. We didn't have to worry about preserving any expensive gowns or fragile nylons, we could let ourselves go. It should have been good, or at least good enough, but it wasn't. As I faced the possibility of inadequacy, a sharp pain stung my lips. Kitty had bitten me. As I recoiled, she hooked a foot behind my ankle and shoved hard. I sat down abruptly on the shaggy rug, which didn't do a great deal to cushion the shock.

"Kitty, what the hell—"

"Stop treating me like a porcelain doll or your baby sister, dammit!" Looking up at her, I had a sudden memory of the slender, fastidious person who'd objected to getting all mussed and excited on a hospital bed, but this wasn't the same girl. She giggled. "It really looks very silly! The ruthless secret agent sitting there with its mouth wide open. . . . Ouch!"

I'd caught an ankle and brought her down beside me. She kicked at me, breaking free, and tried to scramble away, laughing. I grabbed for her and got only a pantaleg and yanked hard on that. Already damaged, it tore further, baring part of a slim, flailing girl-limb. This seemed like a hell of a fine, drunken project, and I proceeded to shuck the leg in question as you'd peel the cornhusk off a tamale. We were both laughing as we struggled breathlessly, both moderately intoxicated and maybe both pretending to be just a little more alcoholically uninhibited than we really were. After all, we had to justify to ourselves and each other our undignified behavior, two grown people roughhousing wantonly and destructively on the floor like a couple of crazy kids. I let the slacks go, half-demolished, and tackled the much flimsier and more satisfactory blouse, feeling her clawing fingers get away with most of my undershirt and some of the skin beneath. . . .

Abruptly, simultaneously, we stopped laughing. I felt her yield, moving against me urgently; I felt myself respond. It took us only a moment to rid ourselves of the tangled wreckage that still obstructed our access to each others' bodies. . . .

FIFTEEN

It was a peaceful awakening. I was lying between clean sheets in a soft bed in a quiet attic room full of diffused daylight and somewhere a girl was singing happily. I felt quite happy, too. I'd survived an endless institutional nightmare, and some fairly violent experiences; but at least I wasn't in an institution any longer. I wasn't anybody's patient any longer except, perhaps, my own.

Of course there were problems. There were still things I was supposed to remember, but to hell with them. You could always make new memories if you misplaced the old ones. . . . I yawned and stretched and got out of the bed and found the bathroom. I grinned at myself in the mirror. I had a slightly swollen lip where she'd bitten me and she'd done a respectable wildcat job on my hide. I wouldn't have believed it if I hadn't been there. My sweet, proper PR lady, for God's sake! Obviously she wasn't even feeling very ashamed of herself or she wouldn't be singing like a bird out in the other room.

There was shaving stuff on the shelf above the washbowl, and a big clean towel by the bathtub. In the bedroom, the contents of my pockets had been piled on the dresser and some fresh clothes that fit me were neatly arranged on one of the chairs. Interesting. Apparently I'd felt enough at home in this apartment before my near-fatal crash to maintain something of a wardrobe here, yet I felt certain that last night was the first time the lady of the house and I. . . . Well, there was no sense in wearing out the mental machinery on a problem the answer to which waited only one room away. When I emerged into the paneled living-dining area, shaved, scrubbed, and respectably attired, Kitty was setting the table for breakfast.

She was wearing slim new blue jeans and a blue-and-white checked gingham shirt with long sleeves. Her long brown hair looked soft and silky. She must have slipped away early from the bed to which we'd finally made our way, and worked hard with shampoo and drier while I slept on. She didn't look around, she didn't even seem to know I was there, but she'd stopped singing. I came up behind her, parted the shining hair and, while she stood quite still by the table, kissed the nape of her neck.

"Miss Davidson, I presume."

"Don't presume too much this morning, my dear," she said quietly. "I think we both presumed quite enough last night."

"Question, ma'am," I said, speaking to the back of her head. "Apparently we've been associated for months on a fairly dangerous mission. A marriage engagement has been mentioned. I even seem to have moved some clothes in here. So how does it happen we never did that before?"

She looked around quickly. "Darling, if I hadn't got quite smashed on two little drinks I'd never have dreamed of doing it last night, and I certainly have no intention of ever doing it again!" She stopped abruptly. Her face grew quite pink. "Well, not *that* way. . . . Oh, damn, something's boiling over."

I grinned, watching her run out of the room, a boyish figure in the brand-new jeans that, indestructible and impenetrable, made it quite clear that the wearer had no intention of cooperating in any undignified sex-shenanigans this morning, no matter what lewd and disgraceful antics she might have participated in last night.

Waiting, I sat down and looked idly out the window at the sunlit suburban view—well, it was about time for a little more sunshine around here. This was only the second time I'd seen blue sky since I'd awakened in the hospital. I could see the freeway embankment up the street, and the tops of the cars and trucks driving by beyond the white-painted barrier up there. It occurred to me that the big highway must have caused a lot of resentment when it was rammed through this peaceful suburb. Even with the windows closed, the steady rumble of traffic was quite audible.

"Your coffee, Monsieur," Kitty said, returning. "What didn't perk all over the stove, that is. You can start on that while I dish up breakfast."

It was very pleasant to tackle a meal that hadn't been prepared in a hospital kitchen and wasn't served by a professional attendant in white. I gave it my full attention for a while, aware that across the table Kitty was also doing justice to her cooking. At last I poured myself another cup of coffee and leaned back comfortably in the chair.

"You didn't answer my question," I said at last. "I mean, you did give me, and those Ministry of Transport investigators, the distinct impression that our relationship was sexy as hell—"

"Oh, that!" She didn't look up from her plate. "I was just following instructions. Mike Ross seemed to think that if I let them, or anybody—there was a microphone in that hospital room, remember—guess that our engagement had been strictly platonic, they'd have realized there was something peculiar going on. Nobody has platonic engagements these days. I guess the man you work for didn't take Mike into his confidence; we didn't know he was going to blow your cover deliberately. And maybe I overdid the brazen-modern-hussy act." She glanced up briefly. "Actually, I wasn't very good, was I? After all the big talk, I couldn't make myself forget about that mike when . . . you came all over amorous that day. Sorry."

I grinned, and stopped grinning. "That Ross guy. I get the impression I don't rate among his very favorite people. Is he jealous or something?"

Kitty looked shocked. "Of you and me? Heavens, no! I'm sure he hasn't the slightest personal interest, at least he's never given me any indication. . . . It's something else, I think. He was very displeased when the U.S. agent assigned to help us—they had to have somebody who wasn't known here in Canada—turned out to be you. Apparently he'd had dealings with you before. Rather unfortunate dealings, I gathered, although he never went into detail."

"I see. An old professional conflict of some kind? I was wondering why he gave me such a hard time last night." I grimaced. "And now let's talk about platonic."

"What?"

"The platonic engagement of Miss Davidson to Mr. Madden, or vice versa," I said. "Platonic. It doesn't sound like me, what little I know about me, And it doesn't sound like what little I know about you, either, if you'll forgive my saying so. And still the two of us are supposed to have lived together in this apartment without—"

She said quickly, "Oh, we weren't really *living* together. You'd just spend the night here when you were up this way on a photo-story, or when you arranged for some other plausible excuse to drive up from Seattle because I'd signaled you—we had a code we used over the phone— that I had something to report. We were together just enough to make our relationship look convincing to anybody who might be checking up on me."

"You mean like your contact with the PPP. Joan Market."

"Yes. We wanted to lay the groundwork, so to speak, so you *could* move in permanently to protect me if things started looking dangerous, without arousing her suspicions. But we didn't want you actually living here until it became necessary—Mike Ross didn't—because we were hoping she might come to see me and we didn't want anybody else here to frighten her away. Mike had somebody watching all the time in the hopes of following her and learning where she was hiding, but she never gave him a chance. She'd been sociable enough back east; but once I moved out here she never came near me. It was all tricky messages and complicated telephone routines, that sort of thing."

"Market. I wonder if that could have been Marquette originally, and what the hell difference it makes." I shook my head. "But you're still dodging, Kitty. Do I gather that all those times I spent the night here I got into my pajamas like a good little boy and retired to the living room couch? And you went into the bedroom and locked the door behind you?" I glanced towards the bedroom door. "I must

106

be more of a gentleman than I thought. It doesn't look like all that much of a lock."

"Gentleman? You were an obstinate mule!" Kitty laughed ruefully. "Of course we got off on the wrong foot. The trouble was, I was warned about you in advance. It seemed I was going to have to play house with a horrible *macho*-gunman type who undoubtedly expected every girl he met to fall swooning into his virile arms. If arms can be virile. Anyway, that was what I was braced for, darling. When the time came, when you came, I was determined not to give you the slightest encouragement. It was all going to be strictly business between us. I made that absolutely clear."

I said, "Obviously, Mr. Ross is never going to be mistaken for John Alden. I'll have to thank him for the great buildup."

She smiled. "Well, as your PR man he does leave something to be desired; but no matter how wonderful you turned out to be, I really wasn't interested—or didn't think I was. I'd just had my heart broken, remember?"

"Sure. Your husband."

"Yes. Roger. Roger Atwell—I kept my maiden name at work after we were married. Actually he broke my heart twice. Once when I learned what he'd got himself mixed up in. I suppose it was selfish, but the fact that he'd let me marry him without telling me, well, it was never quite the same after that. And then, perversely, when he got himself killed it was a terrible wrench just the same. Because he was basically a very nice person in spite. . . ."

"In spite of playing dynamite games with a bunch of fanatics," I said when she stopped.

She nodded gravely. "But it was being such a nice person, such a sensitive person, that got him involved. He couldn't stand all the suffering and oppression he saw, or thought he saw, around him. He felt he had to do something about it. He just did the wrong thing, at least by most people's standards and, as it turned out, by his own. The newspaper stories about the San Francisco explosion upset him terribly. At the time, of course, I didn't understand; I had no idea he had anything to do with those maniacs. But when they actually came to Toronto, where we were living, and told him that now it was his turn as a loyal member of the PPP. . . ." She was silent for a moment. I didn't speak. She went on: "That was when he broke down and told me everything. He said he was going to the police as soon as he learned their plans, but he wanted me to know. . . . He said there was plenty of time to stop it, almost a week, but it was that night the railroad station blew up. He'd thought Dan Market was just taking him there so they could look over the ground and make preparations. Roger was going to tell the authorities the following day; he just wanted to have all the information. . . . I know he wasn't lying to me, I *know* it. They suspected him, they fooled him by giving him the wrong date, they tricked him there and killed him to keep him from betraying them."

She was getting pretty intense about it. I said deliberately, "So you swore revenge and took a vow of chastity; no man should touch you until the PPP had paid for its crimes."

She started to get angry; then she relaxed and made a face at me instead. "It isn't nice to make fun of the girl when she's baring her soul. There wasn't any stupid medieval vow; there was only the simple fact that after going through all *that* I didn't think I'd want to get involved with another man, ever. Well, not for a good many years. And then, gradually, as you turned out to be a good deal more human than I'd expected, your gentlemanly restraint began to seem, well, rather unflattering, if you know what I mean." Her face was pink again. "I knew you were doing it just to be perverse, because I'd hurt your damned little feelings when we'd first met, but just because the girl talks a lot of don't-touch-me nonsense at the start doesn't mean the boy has to keep taking her at her idiot word forever!"

I grinned at her resentful tone. Last night's uninhibited performance began to make more sense. Not only had we both been drinking fairly heavily after a long dry spell, not only had we been feeling strong reactions after our escape from terror and torture, but there had been a lot of old frustrations needing release, even if I couldn't remember them consciously. . . . Well, to hell with the psychological analysis.

"Did you tell anybody that your husband had confessed to you before he was killed?" I asked. "That he'd been planning to go to the cops?"

She shook her head. "No. Not then. Of course Mike Ross got the whole story later when I asked him for help, but at the time I played innocent and ignorant as hard as I could. I was hoping that sooner or later somebody from the PPP would come around to see if I was actually as blind and stupid as I seemed. Of course they didn't have to come around. Joan Market was right there. Once somebody in authority realized that two of the casualties weren't innocent victims like the rest, but had actually been members of the PPP, that put us, the wives, in line for special investigation and questioning, so Joan and I had to spend a lot of time together in a lot of dismal offices and waiting rooms."

"Had you known the Markets before?"

"Oh, no. And Roger hadn't, either, until they made contact with him in Toronto. The PPP has—well, they claim to have—members scattered all over the United States and Canada, but these people act more or less as scouts. Like Roger in Toronto. Then, when the council in Vancouver picks a target, a small strike force moves in and does the actual work with the help of the local member. If you want to call it work. Joan and Dan Market were part of the mobile strike force for the Toronto operation. Of course I didn't learn all that until later."

"How did you get Joan Market to accept you as a recruit?"

"It was more the other way around; she made the first advances," Kitty said. "I made it easy for her with a lot of glib anti-establishment talk. I wanted to see what she would do. When the police couldn't prove anything against either of us and finally let us go, Joan took me out to dinner to celebrate, in a dirty little place where the air was practically solid marijuana smoke. She made the great revelation, watching me closely to see if I showed proper surprise. Naturally, I pretended to be shocked, but not too shocked. It was war, she said, and our husbands had died battling heroically side by side in the front ranks of the fighting underground army, didn't I want to keep his memory bright by taking his place in the great crusade? Once I got over being terribly, terribly hurt at the way Roger had kept his secret from me—to protect me, Joan said—I told her of course I did." Kitty grimaced. "The hardest part was keeping her from knowing that I knew they'd blown my hero-husband into little pieces to keep him quiet."

I frowned. "Did she tell you how her husband came to be killed along with yours?"

"It was apparently an accident. It was a home-made bomb constructed by Dan Market himself, and it exploded prematurely before Dan could leave Roger sitting there on some pretext and sneak off to safety. Of course Joan didn't tell me *that*." Kitty buttered a piece of toast in an absent way. "A few weeks later I got my first instructions from the PPP, meaning Joan. I was to request a transfer to my company's Vancouver office claiming I couldn't stand it any longer in Toronto after everything that had happened. Obviously the PPP wanted to get me away from everybody I knew and out near their headquarters where it was easier for them to watch me closely, just in case I was more clever than I looked. I'll admit I was frightened; I thought there was a good chance they were simply decoying me out here to kill me. That was when I got in touch with Mike Ross, very cautiously. He said for me to do just as Joan said, and he'd find somebody out here to protect me. The rest you know."

"Well, more or less," I said. "Just what the hell kind of cop is this Michael Ross, anyway?"

"He seems to be a fairly highpowered investigator of some kind, although he makes rather a point of referring to himself as a simple policeman." Kitty hesitated. "It's Michel Ross, actually. He says he had a Scottish father and a French mother; but with a striking face like that I'm sure he's part Indian. Not that it matters."

I said, "I thought the Mounties and Indians spent all

their time shooting at each other. Well, it's a crazy, mixed-up world. Is there any more of that coffee?"

She used the last of it to refill my cup, and carried the empty pot out into the kitchen. I watched her go, rather startled to find myself thinking how pleasant it would be to be able to sit like that every morning, watching her. I realized abruptly that I didn't really want my memory back. To hell with the past. Judging by what I'd learned so far, it contained a lot of fairly ugly stuff. I wasn't ashamed of it, somebody always has to do the dirty work, why not me? But everything indicated that I'd put in my time and earned my graduation points. And recently, it seemed, I'd made a serious professional error that had almost got me killed, or at least met a man who was too tough for me. Call it a sign, omen, warning, it wasn't something I could ignore. Quit while you're ahead, I reflected. Quit while you still have a life and somebody to share it with—assuming she's willing, that is.

I watched her return, liking everything I knew about her and wanting to learn more. I'd misjudged her badly at the start. Lovely as she was, fragile as she looked, she'd shot a woman last night for motives she'd considered adequate. She'd watched me kill a man and helped me hide his body. She'd deliberately led us into some fairly undignified sexual behavior for therapeutic reasons. Obviously she wasn't the gentle, civilized young lady she seemed—but with my background, what would I do with a gentle, civilized young lady? This was a real person, not a saccharine dream.

She sat down facing me again, and regarded me a moment with an expression I couldn't read. Abruptly, she said, "I put on fresh coffee for Ross. He ought to be here shortly. When . . . when he gets here, let's tell him we're through, Paul. Finished, fed up, tired of the whole crazy mess."

I still couldn't guess her thoughts. "Why?" I asked.

She said deliberately, "I think that is a very foolish question, darling. You're not a foolish man ordinarily. Or . . . or was it just a relaxing drunken orgy with a cooperative female playmate, exact identity unimportant?"

I studied her for a moment. There was no mistaking

111

her meaning now. I just hadn't let myself believe that her thoughts could be so similar to mine.

I said plaintively, "What happened to all those nice, shy Victorian maidens who waited for the man to do the asking?"

Kitty said unsmiling: "They all got to be old maids sipping sherry on the sly and blubbering into their dainty cambric hankies as they remembered the handsome gentlemen who'd got away from them." She paused, watching me. "*Were* you going to ask?"

I nodded. "But let's approach this sensibly, ma'am. You've just lost one character with blood on his hands —well, at least he was involved with that kind of people. Do you really want to acquire another?"

"You forget, I seem to be slightly homicidal myself," she said steadily. "After last night, I'm hardly in a position to criticize, am I?"

"You're a forward wench," I said. "First you rape me and then you shove a ring on my finger—I assume we are talking rings and such. Well, at least you seem to be willing to make an honest man of me, but what about the Great Davidson Revenge Crusade?"

"I've had all the revenge I need," she said. "I killed one of them stone dead, didn't I? An eye for an eye, a life for a life, and it didn't feel all that good when I did it, not good enough that I care to make a habit of it. As far as I'm concerned, Roger can now rest in peace. As for my duty as a citizen, I've made my public-spirited contribution towards breaking up this gang, haven't I? If Ross and Company can't take it from here, that's their problem. They're paid to do it. I'm not."

"But I am," I said. "At least I assume I am, although I haven't seen any U.S. salary checks lying around."

"People have been known to resign from jobs, even government jobs," she said softly. When I didn't speak, she went on quickly: "I'm not making that a condition. I mean, I'd never try to blackmail a man I . . . a man for whom I had any regard into leaving a career that meant a great deal to him, but does it, darling? Can't you just let that mysterious, unpleasant Mr. Helm stay forgotten? Be Paul Madden. Take good pictures. Marry the girl. . . ."

112

Somebody knocked on the kitchen door. There was a little silence; then the peremptory knock came again.

"Oh, damn, go let the bloody redskin in while I clear the table," Kitty said.

SIXTEEN

"I was against it from the start," Ross said.

I decided that he must definitely have Indian blood, as Kitty had suggested, with his rather broad, brown face dominated by strong cheekbones and a hooked beak of a nose. It was too bad. In addition to our other areas of disagreement, whatever they might turn out to be, it put the barrier of race between us. It didn't mean that I was a better man, or that he was, but it did mean— these strange days when men's differences seem to be considered, proudly, as more important than their similarities—that we'd have trouble understanding each other even if we were willing to try.

"I must tell you, frankly, that I tried very hard to prevent it," he said.

"What you're really saying," I translated, "is that you were against me from the start and tried to prevent me —from doing what?"

Ross started to answer, but stopped as Kitty came into the room with a tray holding three clean cups, a coffee pot, and the customary accessories. He rose from his chair politely. I remained seated on the sofa, just an unmannerly white-eyed crumb of a paleface. We waited while she set steaming cups of coffee around, offered cream and sugar, and sat down beside me.

I said, "You were saying, in effect, that you were opposed to the idea of employing me from the start, Mr. Ross. Why?"

He hesitated, but after a moment he said briskly, "Yes, it's just as well to get the cards on the table, isn't it?

You don't remember, but you've been in Canada before, twice that we're officially aware of. It was my task to clean up after you on the occasion of one of your previous visits, the last one, six or seven years ago."

"Nothing comes back," I said. "Tell me about it."

He sipped coffee from his cup. "There was a two-nation project known as the Northwest Coastal System," he said. "The details don't matter. It's obsolete now, but at the time it was very secret or supposedly so. However, systematic security leaks were detected. We needed a tall man to impersonate a courier on the other side who'd been found dead. The impersonator was to run the courier's route and locate the leaks so we could stop them. You were selected, via computer I believe, partly for your general resemblance to the dead man, but also because you were trained and experienced in certain techniques of survival. Well, you survived, Mr. Helm, but your methods created almost insuperable problems for those of us who were assigned to cover for you in both countries—naturally, publicity was not desired. Speaking only for myself, in one place alone I was confronted by no less than three violently dead bodies for which plausible explanations were required. Granted that you'd been attacked, it seemed like over-reaction. For this reason, when it was suggested that we make use of your services again, my counter-suggestion was that we'd be much better off employing the bubonic plague."

It was a revealing glimpse into my forgotten past. I glanced at Kitty to see how she was taking this gory information about a gent to whom she'd just proposed marriage. She winked at me, the callous wench. It occurred to me that it was also an interesting glimpse into the mind of the man facing me. I suppose it was funny if you looked at it one way—the old frontier way—a red man lecturing a white man on the sanctity of human life. At least that seemed to be more or less what he was saying.

"But you couldn't find any suitable viruses for hire?" I said.

He shrugged. "You were available, right here in the Northwest; a trained agent already in place with a well-established cover. That's a coincidence that still hasn't been explained to my satisfaction, but my superiors refused to look the gift horse in the mouth, as the saying goes. I was ordered to cooperate with you. I've done so to the best of my ability, even though it's just involved covering up another of your one-man massacres. If you read the Vancouver newspapers this morning, you'll learn that an unfortunate schizophrenic ran amok at a local sanitarium last night. Very tragic. The poor fellow has been transferred to an institution for the criminally insane, and the sanitarium's screening and security procedures are being thoroughly investigated. Let's hope the press doesn't stumble onto the fact that our conveniently murderous patient simply doesn't exist."

Kitty said quickly, "You're not being fair! It was hardly a one-man massacre. I . . . I was responsible for one-quarter of it, and I don't apologize for it, Mike."

"Never mind, Kitty," I said. "Mr. Ross and I have simply been clarifying our beautiful relationship. Now we know that he thinks I'm a murderous goon; and I'll put in that I think he's a sentimental schnook. So, having established our basis for mutual respect and cooperation, we can get down to business. Tell me, Ross, what's the People's Protest Party really after?"

After a moment, he laughed shortly. "I suppose that's a reasonably accurate summing-up. As for the triple-initial gang, we don't really know what they want, yet. Presumably, they're still just trying to get our attention. The political demands will come later."

Kitty said, "I'm not so sure they know what they want. I mean, it's a vague, violent sort of religion, actually. I got the feeling from Joan Market that a lot of them were protesting without knowing exactly what they were protesting against, and certainly not what they were protesting for."

"Yes, that's what makes them so dangerous," Ross said. "Palestinian or Irish terrorists are bad enough, but everybody knows what they're fighting for, more or less. Most ordinary people aren't interested in dying, or killing, for those particular causes. This mystical-violent protest group, with its still unspecified goals, is a different matter entirely. It seems to attract just about any unbalanced

116

person with a grievance against society, as well as some more-or-less well-meaning crusaders for social justice like Miss Davidson's late husband. The unfortunate fact seems to be that there are a good many people around these days who'd simply like to blow things up. All they need is somebody to show them how and tell them it's quite the proper thing to do."

He'd summed it up very neatly. Aside from the fact that he didn't like me, he seemed like a fairly reasonable and intelligent guy.

I asked, "How many incidents have been traced to them so far? The only definites I've heard or read about are the recent explosion at Tsawwassen, the San Francisco blast and the Toronto job where Atwell and Market died. The paper I read speculated about some others, but they obviously weren't sure."

"They're always speculating," Ross said dryly. "Naturally, since publicity is what the PPP obviously wants, the official policy—very unpopular with the press—has been to deny it to them as much as possible. There have definitely been five others, making eight in all. Forty-seven people have died to date, including two known members of the PPP."

I said, "On both sides of the border, I understand."

"Yes. Three bangs above and five below, if you want the exact distribution."

"And the terrorist headquarters, at least until last night, was at Inanook?"

He hesitated. "In a manner of speaking. We've found some hidden arms, and there's evidence that the remoter parts of the grounds had been used for guerilla-type training of some kind. However, your experience and what we've picked up from the personnel that didn't get away —unfortunately, the guard who escaped you seems to have had time to warn a number of key people—indicates that the real administrative functions are located elsewhere in this area."

I grinned. "You can't have it both ways, *amigo*."

"What do you mean?"

"First you gripe about my killing too many people, and then you gripe about my not killing enough. I let the guard, Frechette, escape instead of drilling him through the head, as I should have. That's what you're saying, isn't it?" He didn't speak at once, and I went on quickly, "Did you ever find that limousine driver, Gavin Lewis?"

"Yes," said Ross. "We found him. Unfortunately, somebody else had found him first."

"Dead?"

"Sitting in his Mercedes with most of his head blown off by a twelve-bore shotgun. Rather a mess, as you can imagine."

I said, "That seems to indicate he had something to tell us. Like for instance the address at which he regularly picked up the little round guy who was so interested in my interrogation. John Ovid. Any information on Ovid yet?"

"So far, none."

"What about that interesting connection between the pilot, Herb Walters, and Emilio Brassaro? Has anybody figured out how a New York syndicate bigshot figures in all this?"

Ross shook his head. "All we have so far are guesses."

I frowned. "What about Walters? Was he just employed as a pilot back east or did he have other duties? I got the impression that he was a little more than just a fly-boy on Brassaro's payroll."

Ross laughed shortly. "Quite a bit more. He was a fairly unsavory character altogether, with a reputation for being as expert with firearms as he was with aircraft."

"A handy dual-purpose fellow for a guy like Brassaro to keep around," I said a bit grimly. "When you weren't using him for a hit with his gun, you could always send him and his plane to Mexico or Colombia for a load of grass or something stronger. But he doesn't sound like the socially conscious sort of chap who'd join the PPP to clean up the world, yet he seems to have been in on all their secrets, including the details of their next action, scheduled soon. Do we have anything on that?"

Ross shook his head. "Not unless you've remembered something significant."

"Sorry, that last flight is still a total blank, along with a lot of other stuff. If anything comes, I'll let you know."

"Yes," Ross said, "we'd like you to do that." He reached for his wallet and brought out a card. "Call that number, please. If I'm not there, the message will be forwarded."

"Sure." I put the card away, watching him.

He spoke deliberately, "In view of your amnesia, we felt we owed you this conversation, Mr. Helm. We would not want to withhold any information that might help you regain your memory, for our sakes as well as yours. Since we asked for your help, we're also obliged to protect you with regard to last night's killings—you and Miss Davidson both. However, if you don't mind, we'll handle the rest of this terrorist problem, at least on our side of the border, in our own gentle and ineffectual way."

I nodded slowly, still watching him. "You've discussed this with Washington, of course."

"Yes. Your chief says it's entirely up to us. We asked for an agent with certain qualifications, and he was instructed to supply one. If said agent is no longer required here, I was told, there is plenty of other work for him to do. Your chief said to tell you that you can take a few days to catch your breath, but that he expects you in Washington within the week." Ross waited for me to say something. When I didn't, he went on, a little embarrassed: "We're not telling you you must leave town on the noon stagecoach, you understand. That would be very rude and ungrateful in view of the sufferings you've endured on our behalf. However, it would please us to see you wind up your business in Canada as quickly as possible. In the meantime, we'll appreciate it very much if you leave our business strictly alone."

I glanced towards Kitty and asked, "What about her?"

"We're grateful for her help to date, but her cover is blown," Ross said. "Of course there's no question of asking her to leave the country. She's in a slightly different category, wouldn't you say? However, from now on this case is no longer any of her concern."

I studied his face for a moment longer. "If we leave your business strictly alone, can you guarantee that your business will leave us strictly alone?"

He frowned briefly. "Oh, I see what you mean. Yes,

I'll take steps to make certain of that, of course."

There was another small silence. I got up, watching him rise to face me rather warily, as if he wasn't quite sure what my answer to his ultimatum would be or how I would express it.

I said, "Okay, you've got a deal."

We listened to the traffic on the freeway for a moment. Ross cleared his throat. "Well, in that case. . . . Thank you for the coffee, Miss Davidson. I can find my own way out."

She rose. "I'll see you to the door."

We all moved into the kitchen a bit awkwardly, in silence. With his hand on the knob of the outer door, Ross turned.

"Mr. Helm—"

I grinned at him. "Don't bother, *amigo*. The warning isn't necessary."

"What—"

"You're uneasy because it was too easy," I said. "You expected me to kick and scream, so now I've got you worried. The old suspicious-cop syndrome." I set my empty cup, that I was still holding, on the kitchen counter. "Now you want to tell me that if I'm pulling a fast one, just pretending to play along with you, I'll regret it. For instance, those three dead men at Inanook might come back to haunt me. Right?"

He smiled faintly. "A mind reader, Mr. Helm?"

I was aware of Kitty standing there, but I didn't look at her. I said, without smiling back, "I'd better explain it to you so you won't get nervous, Ross. Nervous gents with official connections give me the willies. To make sure you're nice and relaxed, I'll tell you that Kitty and I were discussing it just before you arrived." I felt her stir, but I kept my eyes on Ross, and continued speaking: "The fact is, I seem to have lost a lot of bad memories. We were considering the possibility of, let's say, replacing them with nothing but good ones, together. I hope I'm making myself clear. I'll have to thrash it out with Washington, of course. Apparently I've worked with that guy long enough that if he needs me for something specific, memory or no memory, I can't just walk out on him

120

without notice. But as far as you're concerned, you haven't got a thing to worry about as far as I'm concerned. Okay?"

Ross looked at us for a moment. "I see. My congratulations, Mr. Helm, and my best wishes to both of you."

He threw a final glance at Kitty as he went out. It was obvious that he was having a hard time maintaining a diplomatic silence. We listened to his footsteps going down the outside stairs. We heard the car drive away. I looked at Kitty at last, standing beside me. It gave me a funny feeling in my throat to look at her. There was no reason to cry about it, of course, but she was really a hell of a pretty girl. I guess you'd call it love. She was watching me gravely, with a faint question in her eyes.

I said, "He thinks you're making a terrible mistake. He thinks you're much too good for a dreadful fellow like me. Of course he's perfectly right."

The question went away. She laughed softly and came into my arms.

SEVENTEEN

It was a public phone in a busy department store in West Vancouver called Eaton's; a branch, I gathered, of a larger store downtown. What with the inevitable rain that had replaced the morning's sunshine, it was already getting dark outside. The place was full of last-minute shoppers picking up last-minute items on their way home from work. Preparing for what I hoped would be my final report on this mission—I wanted to wrap it up neatly as much for my benefit as that of the man in Washington— I'd spent most of the day trying to figure things out logically since I couldn't remember them, while Kitty stayed carefully out of my way, smart girl. Perhaps I'd also been delaying my long-distance confrontation with Mac because I didn't expect it to be easy. My impression was that, working for certain types of organizations, you didn't just pick up your marbles and go home when you happened to feel like it. . . .

Finally, I'd borrowed Kitty's car, a sporty little Toyota with a flashy stripe down the side, and gone for a long drive up the coast by myself. I'd been curious about whether or not I'd have a bodyguard watching over me— I did—but I suppose I'd also hoped that the sight of a lot of Canadian salt water and rocks and pine trees might trigger something in my obstinate memory. It hadn't worked. Now I listened to the ringing of the phone on the other side of the continent. The ringing stopped. I heard Mac's voice.

"Yes?"

"Eric here." I found myself using the code name he'd

mentioned at the start of our previous phone conversation.

"I hope you're happy in your retirement, Eric."

Well, at least I wouldn't have to break that news myself. I said sourly, "Quick-dial Ross, the fastest phone in the West. Incidentally, he's got a tail on me for protection until I get out of here, but I don't suppose the guy's above picking up any information that comes his way. However, this pay phone ought to be safe, if it matters. Did you actually tell Ross, earlier, to ship me back to Washington if he didn't want me here? He says you did."

"His statement is correct."

I said without expression, "I thought this was supposed to be an international operation. How come you're letting those crummy Canucks shove us around like that, sir?" When he didn't speak, I went on: "Or could it be that you're just as happy to have me booted out of here because, although I got drafted for some extra bodyguard duty because I was handy, my real mission here is actually finished?"

The phone was silent for several seconds longer. At last the calm voice three thousand miles away said, "Perhaps. But we have no confirmation, have we?"

"You mean that Walter Christofferson, alias Herbert Walters, may come strolling out of the bush any day with his parachute on his shoulder?"

Mac said softly, "Amnesia, Eric?"

I said, "I've lost my memory, sir. I haven't lost my cottonpicking mind. The fact that you're willing to have me come home now, I figure, indicates that I've actually accomplished more or less what I was sent up here to do. Well, what *have* I accomplished here besides a cracked head? It's pretty obvious, isn't it? My only other accomplishment of record, at least up to last night when I kind of shook things loose out at Inanook with Kitty's help, is that I took a certain bush pilot with a very peculiar background out into the boondocks and lost him, whether temporarily or permanently remains to be seen." I paused. When no response came through the telephone, I said, "And the motive behind the removal, sir, at least initially, had nothing whatever to do with terrorism or the PPP."

That got a reaction. "I'd like to hear the reasoning that led you to this conclusion."

I said, "Well, you told me last night that the agent with whom I was originally working, Sally Wong, took orders from elsewhere, and I got a distinct impression you didn't mean Mr. Ross and his Canadian associates. And then, of course, there was that very elaborate photographic cover I'd been given."

Mac said quickly, "There was nothing wrong with your cover until I decided to break it for strategic reasons. Nothing at all."

I'd touched his professional pride. I grinned at the wall of the phone cubicle. It was nice to catch him acting slightly human for a change.

"Absolutely nothing," I agreed. "My cover was airtight, watertight, bulletproof, and non-magnetic. It was totally impermeable and impenetrable. That's just the point." Well, a couple of doctors had seen through it, at least part way, but I decided not to mention that.

"Please explain," Mac said.

"It was too damned good, sir," I said. "It was much better than it had to be. You'd made absolutely certain I wouldn't be revealed as a government agent no matter what happened. You'd even reprogrammed the official computers to spit out Madden data in response to Helm stimuli. All this for the benefit of a bunch of dynamite-freaks who probably wouldn't know how to get any information out of Washington that wasn't in the phone book? It didn't make sense, sir. It was overkill in spades."

"What conclusion did you draw?"

I said, "The only possible answer, sir, was that you or someone from whom you were getting your instructions had a project going we were all a bit ashamed of. Ironclad precautions were being taken to make certain there'd be no kickback under any conceivable or inconceivable circumstances. Well, what could we possibly do to a gang of murdering bomb-maniacs that we'd have to be ashamed of if the story got out? I mean, short of gratuitous torture and mutilation? I understand the Israelis practically went to war to deal with one bunch, and most of the uninvolved world just cheered. If that had been my original mission here, to get very tough with the PPP, my fancy background would have been a complete waste of time. As long as the bombings get stopped, the general public won't give a damn what methods are used."

Mac said carefully, "As you say, memory apart, there seems to be nothing much wrong with your cottonpicking mind. Go on."

"Terrorists scare people," I said. "For terrorism, they're willing to make exceptions. They'll condone official acts they'd never sanction if perpetrated in the line of ordinary intelligence-gathering or law-enforcement operations, these post-Watergate days. But suppose they learned that a certain law-enforcement branch of the U.S. government had borrowed a trained weapons specialist from an agency more closely related to intelligence to brutally remove in cold blood an individual who was simply frustrating their efforts to get the legal goods on said individual's boss. . . . You did say Brassaro was in the import business, meaning drugs, didn't you?"

"I did."

"What happened?" I asked. "Did somebody jump to conclusions when Emilio sent his top soldier out here to play bush pilot? Did they figure that, not satisfied with his usual Caribbean delivery routes, he was setting up a new, roundabout pipeline by way of the Pacific Coast and Canada? And did they then decide that the best way of putting a stop to the new project was to put a stop to Christofferson himself, which had the added advantage of getting the guy out of the way for good? And if so, what the hell are we doing, running homicidal errands for a bunch of pot-cops? Is that our regular line of work, sir?"

"Not pot, Eric," Mac said mildly. "The syndicate, to use the popular name, has never been greatly interested in marijuana; the amateur competition is too great and the product is too bulky." He paused as if for comment, but I let the silence ride. He went on: "Where drugs are concerned, some people seem to lose all perspective. One cannot argue with these crusaders against chemical evil; and there is nothing more dangerous than a frustrated crusader. They had been getting nowhere trying to build a case against Brassaro. Any time an investigator or informer would seem to promise real evidence, he would either disappear, or be found dead, or he would decide that he'd been mistaken and had no useful information after all. But then Christofferson was sent west, and they started making some progress. The protective organization did not function nearly so well without him; obviously he was the key man. Add the threat of a flood of narcotics from a new direction. . . . As you have guessed, they came to us."

I said sourly, "I don't mean to be critical, sir, but I was kidding myself that this dirty-tricks outfit of ours—that's what we are, isn't it?—had something to do with the national security. I don't feel too damned happy about getting concussion, almost dying of exposure, and losing my memory, just to make life easy for a bunch of narcs, even pretty little ones like Miss Wong—"

I stopped. He was laughing. Although I couldn't remember anything about him, I had a feeling this was not a common occurrence.

"What's so funny, sir?" I asked.

"That is the second time I've heard that speech, Eric," he said. "You used practically the same words when I first described the mission to you."

"What did you say to change my mind?"

"I mentioned a code name. Norma."

"Who's Norma?"

"You have the tense wrong. Norma was one of our people. You knew her quite well. But of course this organization does not countenance personal vendettas, so when Norma died in South America because a triggerhappy drug buyer thought her mission there might conflict with his profits—the supplier had other interests that had brought him to our attention—we did nothing but enter the man's name in a certain file, let's call it the opportunity file. You understand, we do not normally indulge in retribution of any kind. If somebody is killed in the line of duty by a legitimate opponent, that is all in the day's work. However, as a matter of self-preservation, we do try to discourage stray thugs from interfering with our people in a fatal way. We still do not go after them on our own initiative except in very flagrant cases, but if the opportunity should be offered to us we may, for instance, accept a mission we would otherwise have refused. That is why it's called the opportunity file."

"Norma," I said thoughtfully. "Nothing comes. How well did I know her?"

"You worked with her on two different Mexican assignments," Mac said. "You spent some leave with her down there after the last one. Her real name was Virginia Dominguez, if that helps."

I shook my head, and remembered he couldn't see me, a continent away. "It doesn't," I said. I wanted to ask more questions about Virginia Dominguez alias Norma. It seemed inconsiderate of me not to remember her, particularly since she was dead. However, other matters had priority. "What you're saying is that Christofferson killed Norma to clear the way for one of his narcotics runs for Brassaro. That's why we agreed to help Sally Wong's people by taking him out. To let the syndicate boys know that when they see our people using the sidewalk it's real smart of them to step off into the gutter where they belong, right?"

"Or, as I said on another occasion, Eric, they have to learn not to monkey with the buzzsaw when it's busy cutting wood."

"Sure. But after all that soul-searching, we eventually learned that Christofferson, or Walters, wasn't out here for narcotics purposes after all. Wong spotted him with the wicked widow, Joan Market, thus tying him to the terrorist PPP. In the meantime I'd been ordered to transfer my romantic attentions from one girl to another; but finally, I suppose, I got the green light on Walters—somebody figured we knew all we needed about the guy and it was time for him to go. Kitty was back in the East on business and I could take care of Walters before she got back. Only he was a little better than we'd expected or I was a little worse. I wound up in a hospital. However, he still hasn't shown, so maybe I managed to muddle through to a measure of success, anyway." I hesitated. "Under the circumstances, this is mere curiosity, but did you manage to dig up anything on the names I gave you? Gavin Lewis, I've already heard about; Ross told

127

me about finding him dead. What about Ovid?"

I'd thought he might get stuffy about discussing such information with an agent who'd declared his intention of resigning, but he answered readily enough: "John Ovid we have traced. He is an expert who has been lent to Emilio Brassaro by a St. Louis business associate named Renfeld, Otto Renfeld. Your little round man is named Heinrich Glock, known as Heinie the Clock, perhaps for his regular and reliable ways with firearms." Mac hesitated. "Incidentally, Mr. Ross reports that all the security guards at the Inanook Sanitarium seem to have gone underground. He tried to round them up for questioning but not a single one, regular or substitute, could be found."

I said, "My error, sir. The one who escaped, Frechette, must have given the scramble signal the minute he found a phone. What about Mrs. Market? Any signs of her?"

"None whatever. She seems to be a very elusive lady. And I should tell you that Dr. Albert Caine is also missing. He eluded surveillance only a few hours ago, however, so it may not be part of the general exodus."

"I didn't gather there was a great deal of trust going between him and the PPP," I said. "It seems unlikely that he'd go to them for shelter, or that they'd give it to him if he did. Most likely he's just bailed out to save his own skin. Do we have any idea where the rest are likely to have holed up?"

"Not yet."

"How many guards are we talking about, anyway? I could never get a clear picture in that place. They came and went."

"The total roster is about fifteen. We're not certain about the current status of some of the listed substitutes."

I said, "That's a nice little strong-arm squad if somebody wants to use it. Ross said they'd been practicing guerilla tactics on the back lot. He also said he'd found some firearms, but he didn't say how many they'd got away with, or what kind." I grimaced. "Talking about firearms, what weapons does Ovid have such regular and reliable ways with? Does he pop them over the horizon or does he blast them face to face?"

Mac spoke evenly, "For a man about to go into civilian life, you ask a lot of questions, Eric."

He was perfectly right, of course. I was finding myself oddly reluctant to bring the conversation to an end. After all, if my understanding was correct, I had worked for this man and his agency for a good many years, maybe most of my adult life.

Before I could speak, Mac went on: "Glock is said to be fairly versatile. He had sniper training in the armed forces. For close range he prefers a twelve-gauge shotgun. Number One buckshot when he can get it; and apparently it is available up there or he brought his own. That chauffeur, Lewis, had his head blown off by such a load."

I said, "With a buckshot specialist who can also handle a sniper's rifle prowling the local mists with a tough gang of armed mercenaries, I'd say it's a hell of a good time for me to pull out, wouldn't you, sir? He might run out of limousine drivers and come after me."

Mac disregarded this. He said, "Let me titillate your active curiosity with another piece of information. We recently received a very interesting report concerning the explosive devices employed by the PPP or, rather, the means used to detonate them."

I frowned at a pretty girl with an armload of packages heading for the department store doors.

"Interesting?" I said. Mac waited, obviously testing me a little, which gave me the cue. I said, "I don't think I'm very interested in whether they used an hour glass, or an alarm clock, or some fancy gizmo involving the speed with which a certain acid eats through a certain metal. Should I be, sir? What I mean is, the only thing that would really interest me, in connection with detonators, would be learning that they didn't use a timer at all. Now *that* I'd find fascinating."

Mac said softly, "Very good, Eric."

I frowned. "Don't tell me. Let me guess. A remote-control device?"

"So we're told. You see the implications, of course."

I said, "I see that these threepee characters must be even nuttier than I thought. Instead of using a tick-tock detonator that lets them get well clear after planting the boom-stuff, they've got a radio contraption that necessitates their remaining within firing distance, whatever it may be, waiting to push a little red button. Screwy!" I started to ask another question, but stopped and said suspiciously, "For a man about to accept my resignation, you're handing out a lot of very confidential dope, sir. At least I don't suppose this has been announced in the press."

There was a little pause. At last Mac said, "Nobody resigns from this agency, Eric, in the strict sense of the word. Apparently that is among the things you have forgotten."

I said, "I see." It seemed like a safe thing to say, even though it wasn't exactly true.

He let me wait another few seconds, then he said: "However, you may request inactive status if you like. I'd rather you didn't; that is why I've answered all your questions and added a few additional facts I thought you might find professionally intriguing."

"Why?" I asked.

"What?"

"Why would you rather I didn't request inactive status, sir? I goofed, didn't I? Walters almost got me. For all we know, he may even have managed to get away. And now I've managed to get myself declared *persona non grata* by a friendly neighboring country. Seems like you'd be happy to retire a guy with a record like that." He didn't say anything. I watched the wet people coming in out of the rain, shaking themselves off; and the dry people heading out into the rain, buttoning themselves up. Mac was still waiting. I said, "Okay, it's a girl, sir."

"I see. Ross didn't mention that. Miss Davidson?"

"Yes. She doesn't make it a condition, but she'd prefer it. Her preferences are . . . fairly important to me, sir. Particularly since I'm not a bit sure I wouldn't prefer it, too."

"Without memory, you can't be certain what you prefer, can you, Eric?" When I didn't answer, he went on, "It doesn't have to be field duty. Not that I have any doubts on that score; we may not know how you managed with

130

Walters, if you did, but we do know that your performance at Inanook was quite satisfactory regardless of what Mr. Ross may say. However, if the lady would rather have you spending more time at home, and if she has no objection to residing in Washington. . . ." He hesitated, and went on: "This is no longer an easy agency for one man to supervise. I have been looking for someone to share the responsibility. Preferably a man who has been with us a very long time. Like you."

It was startling; it was flattering; but it was also a bit embarrassing. Here was a man whom I wouldn't recognize on the street, who'd apparently thought enough of me before my plane crash to plan on making me his second in command whenever I decided to retire from field work—it seemed unlikely that the idea had come to him on the spur of the moment. In spite of my current medical problems, he was ready to go through with the plan. There was even a hint that he'd be grooming me as his successor. . . .

"You put me on kind of a spot, sir," I said.

"I hope so." After a little, he said, "You may want to consult the lady."

"No. I know what she'd say. She's had enough of the exciting life of the undercover operative. She wants out. For both of us."

"And you, Eric?"

I was grateful for my loss of memory. Under other circumstances, I might have felt that I was betraying a friendship, or at least a working association, of long standing. Even without remembrance, it wasn't a comfortable moment—but I concentrated on a mental picture of a slim girl in jeans and a gingham shirt singing to herself as she set the breakfast table.

"I want out, too."

"Very well, Eric." His voice was expressionless. "Let me just remind you that the decision is not, at this end, irreversible. Meanwhile, your request for inactive status will be approved if you choose to make it."

I made it.

EIGHTEEN

Outside, it was night. Mist made dandelion-haloes around the parking-lot lights and a steady drizzle was falling. As I drove away, I was aware of Ross's man trailing along behind in an undernourished-looking Japanese station wagon. It occurred to me that it would be pleasant to live in a manner that didn't necessitate forever watching the mirrors to see what was coming up astern, except in a peaceful, traffic-conscious way. Well, I was committed now. I was going to give it a try.

I didn't think Mac really expected me to succeed. *The decision is not, at this end, irreversible.* He'd done his best to stop me, he'd made it quite clear that I was welcome back, all of which was comforting to the ego; but I had a distinct feeling that he was used to agents dropping out to try the peaceful life, and I didn't have him too worried. Maybe they even ran office pools there in Washington on how long it would be before good old X-14 or Q-36 returned to the fold, bored stiff.

I didn't think I'd be bored stiff. So far, of the brief life I could remember—omitting a few pleasant youthful recollections—about half of it had been spent in a hospital, and the other half in the violent ward of a booby hatch partly converted to other uses. It was time for a change. I wanted a world where a gun was something you picked up only when you wanted to match wits with a duck; a steady ordered world in which you delivered your photographic efforts to the client on time and then drove home to find martinis in the pitcher and dinner in the oven. . . .

Dinner was in the oven, all right. I could smell roast beef as I stepped through the kitchen door. The martinis weren't mixed yet, but gin, vermouth, and Scotch had been set out on the counter, plus a little jar of olives, a pitcher, and the appropriate glasses. There were two other glasses as well, with hollow stems. I grinned, remembering my thought that she was basically a chiffon-and-champagne girl. I peeked into the refrigerator, or fridge as Kitty liked to call it in her Canadian-British way, and there was the bubble-stuff, cooling. Moving into the other room, I found candles on the table set for two by the window. Her intention was obvious. After our undignified wrestling match on the living room floor, she wanted to show me that there were more gracious and pleasant ways of achieving the same object.

"Kitty," I called, expecting an answer from the bedroom where she'd gone, presumably, to change into something nice and glamorous after making the dinner preparations in her jeans. There was no answer.

I stood inside the living room doorway for a moment, frowning. I took a step forward, and an odd glint of light from one of the windowpanes caught my eye. Instinct made me step back quickly; instinct made me reach for a weapon I didn't have. Cautiously, I sidled around the room towards the dining nook, feeling naked and vulnerable and suddenly very scared, but not for myself. I kept out of range of the window until, from a safe angle, I could see it clearly: the single, small, starred bullet-hole a little off-center in the dark, rain-spotted glass.

I looked down at last. I knew what I would see, and she was lying there, of course. The one-shot boys don't miss. There wasn't any immediate shock. My mind just went coldly to work on it. He'd apparently got her as she stepped to the window to pull the curtains. A .30-caliber rifle, I judged, fired from the freeway embankment up the street. Probably, they'd used a van and pulled out on the shoulder up there, feigning engine or tire trouble. A van because you can't see into it much. He'd have arranged himself comfortably in front, the little round man who was reliable as a clock; and he'd have used the vehicle's windowsill for a rest. Two hundred yards give or take twenty. Telescopic sight. At that range, not long for a trained sniper, it could have been done with iron sights, but these optical days there isn't a rifleman in a thousand who knows how.

Ovid hadn't gambled. He was a pro. He hadn't fired while she was moving around the table attending to the last-minute details. He'd known she would come to the window to close things up as darkness fell, giving him a perfect target, and she had. I remembered waiting like that once in a Central American jungle; waiting for my target to step into the clear and stand perfectly still because you don't try for moving targets at five hundred meters. I remembered. . . . Remembered?

Crazy things were suddenly happening in my head. I stood there looking down at the slender body in a hostess garment that was long and pink and filmy—slightly disordered now as she lay half-curled up, half-concealed by the tablecloth. I saw the small pink slippers, and the small pale face, and the blood, but I wasn't really there. I was in a hundred other places. They came and they went: the places and the people. It was all there, but it was going by too fast for me to study it, like a film spliced by an idiot and projected by a maniac. I remembered. . . .

The projector stopped. Everything came to a sudden halt. There had been a dull, hard sound outside. *Stupid,* I told myself sharply, *they wouldn't stop with her*: *if they wanted her they'd want you, too.*

I knew exactly what the sound had been. My bodyguard had just left us. Maybe he'd simply been shot; maybe he'd managed to get off a hopeless shot of his own—a warning to me, perhaps—as they sneaked up on him silently, possibly while he bent over the body of his colleague, the man Ross would have left to protect the house, who'd undoubtedly been taken out earlier, before the rifleman moved into position. In any case, my shadow was gone. I knew it as surely as if another dead body had been placed at my feet.

Now they'd be coming for me. Not Ovid. He was a pro. They'd have wanted him to try for me when I returned to the apartment, and he'd have refused. Even if he'd been willing to hang around after his first shot, trusting that the freeway noise had masked the report, he wouldn't tackle a running shot at a long-legged gent loping through the rain between car and house on a dark night. With a scope-sighted rifle under those conditions you couldn't even see the crosshairs. And even with his shotgun, he wouldn't participate in a clumsy frontal attack. He'd consider himself a surgeon, not a butcher; brute force was out of his line. He'd done his part, had Ovid. The rest was up to the ex-Inanook guards. Fifteen men, Mac had said, and one woman if she liked to participate in that sort of thing. . . .

Call it instinct, call it experience—the experience that was just coming back to me in a wildly confused and disorganized way. I knew they were out there. I knew they were coming in. I didn't try to kid myself I might have heard an auto crash on the freeway, or a neighbor trying to replace a burned-out porch light and dropping the bulb. It didn't occur to me to try the fire-escape at the bedroom end of the house. For one thing, they'd have it covered, and for another, I wasn't in a running mood. I looked down briefly, call it a farewell glance if you like, and went to meet them.

They were on the outside stairs when I grabbed the knives out of the rack: the two big chef's knives I'd spotted the first time I'd walked through. People are always helping themselves to your guns in this world; it seems to make them feel moral as hell. You learn to keep your eyes open for other weapons. There was one eight-inch Sabatier and one ten-incher, a real sword. Both had wicked, heavy, sharp triangular blades that were wasted on vegetables. They were at the door; they kicked it in. They came through it movie-style, two of them, waving submachineguns, for God's sake! They were really taking their protest movement seriously.

I recognized the nearest; I'd seen him before in uniform, at Inanook, making the outside rounds. I threw the big knife point-first, letting it slip off my fingers; there wasn't room to put a spin on it at that close range. It flew like a spearhead without the shaft and went hilt-deep into the chest. The chopper, to use the old Al Capone term

135

that has nothing to do with helicopters, which hadn't been invented then, clattered on the floor. As the man sagged aside, I threw the eight-incher. It got the throat of the guy beyond, a little higher than I'd intended, but why should I admit that? It looked very good, very impressive, very calculated.

That was the idea now, to make it look good. Somebody once called it the death run. The theory is very simple. When the odds are overwhelming and retreat is cut off, when there's no place left to go or you just don't care to go there, that's the time you let the word get around once more that none of us comes cheap. They can have us any time, but they've got to pay the price. The tariff is more than a lot of people can afford. It makes things a little safer for those left behind. Just like the opportunity file, it instills a little respect for the outfit that may save another agent's life at a later date. Not that I was worrying about respect, or safety, with Kitty Davidson dead in the next room.

I dove for the submachinegun on the floor. With that, I could hose them out of the doorway and off the stairs like dirt. I might even be able to shoot my way clear if I wanted to, but I didn't want to. I was doing fine right there, or would be if I could just get my hands on the goddamned chopper, and if they'd just keep coming to me like good little terrorists. I had a grip on the weapon, I was turning it around to fire, when a gun crashed in the doorway and the room kind of exploded and went dark. I went away, but not all the way away. I could hear them arguing above me.

A man wanted to kill me, or finish killing me. It seemed like a very intelligent idea, from his point of view. I'd heard his voice before but I couldn't remember where. A woman said no. I didn't recognize her voice. She used some very unladylike words. As she stood over me protectively, her long skirt brushed my face. I was all for the man. He was only showing good common sense. I'd have killed me, if I'd been in his place. I'd got five of them so far and I was proud of it. I'd damned well get some more if they let me live, all of them if I could, down to the women and children, the dogs and cats and pet parakeets, and he knew it.

I felt very objective about it. I was entirely on his side, he had all the best and most professional arguments, but the woman won.

NINETEEN

I woke up remembering, but it wasn't all that great. Of course I had a tremendous, thundering headache that prevented me from enjoying my newfound memories in full. However, the fact was that except for a few scraps of information of current interest, I hadn't really missed any of the stuff badly while it was gone.

The psychiatrist at the hospital, Lilienthal, had told me that would be the case, when he was trying to reassure me about my amnesia shortly after I'd been delivered to his doorstep by helicopter express. He'd explained that, as a rule, the condition bothers other people more than it does the patient. They tend to consider him a weird medical curiosity; he just thinks of himself as a perfectly normal guy who's got a slight gap in his recollections, which he soon learns to live with. . . .

"Matt."

It was a girl's voice, slightly and intriguingly accented. For a moment I knew a surge of incredulous hope; then I knew it wasn't *that* girl's voice, I'd never hear that again. This was a different accent, not Canadian but very faintly oriental.

"Matt, or Paul, or whatever you're calling yourself now, wake up, damn you! Eric? Come on, snap out of it. I'm going nuts cooped up in here with a lousy corpse. *Please* wake up!"

It wasn't exactly Far East verbiage; but the face I saw, and recognized, when I opened my eyes, was Asiatic enough although it was liberally streaked with occidental dirt. At least I didn't think I'd been transplanted halfway around the world while I was out. I licked my dry lips. I wanted to ask what the hell she was doing here, wherever here was, but the question didn't come out that way, maybe because in spite of my shiny and efficient new memory I had a moment's difficulty recalling her name.

"Who . . . what corpse?"

"Well, when they dumped you in here, I was sure you were dead!"

"In where?"

My eyes were starting to pick up details beyond her, but there wasn't much to see. At first glance, it seemed to be a dim, cold, empty void of a place, like a cellar, illuminated only by a round skylight forming part of a trapdoor giving access from above. An iron ladder led up to the trapdoor. There were certain rippling watery sounds, however, and some uneasy hints of movement, that cast doubt upon the cellar theory.

"I don't know where," said the girl leaning over me. "I was on the floor of the car with somebody's feet on me all the time we were driving. Some kind of crummy barge tied to a falling-down dock on a very muddy river. Close to flood stage with all the rain, I think. A couple of other boats tied up at a nearby float; very funny-looking, beat-up old boats. A boom to hold some logs. Lots of current farther out, if it matters. There seemed to be all kinds of stuff drifting by out there, everything from beer cans to telephone poles. A high rocky shore. A little rocky island to shelter this half-ass harbor or whatever you want to call it. The moon peeked out for a moment just as they were bringing me aboard in the dark. We're up front, in the cargo hold or whatever you call it. The barge has a goodsized house or cabin at the back, but it looks like a do-it-yourself project. Not a real pilot-house, if you know what I mean. I saw only three men but there could be more. I saw one woman— that unwashed Market bitch with her symbolic Afro and her so-casual horseblanket and her long, frayed denim skirt. Firearms galore, including some very nasty little full-automatic numbers, straight magazines, skeleton stocks." She stopped briefly to catch her breath. "End of situation report, sir. At your service, sir. Questions, sir?"

I grinned painfully. "Hello, Wong," I said.

"Wrong Chinese girl, sah," she said, burlesquing the accent. "Me not Lo Wong, me Sally Wong. Lo Wong my sister. . . . Ouch, that's pretty corny, isn't it? I must be scared or something. And talking about unwashed bitches, I wonder what they used this hold for before it became a detention cell. Or maybe I'd rather not know." She grimaced, pushing her short black hair back from her dirty face. "Darling, we simply must stop meeting like this. A hospital room, a rusty barge. . . . I thought that was a pretty good act I put on for you at that hospital. Poignant. Touching. Remember?"

Her voice was a little breathless. It obviously meant a great deal to her to have somebody to talk to at last. It couldn't have been fun, being locked up in the dark for hours with a man she thought dead.

"I remember," I said. "What's a Blossom?"

"What?"

"Operation Blossom," I said. "According to our mutual friend, Herbert Walters, that great frontier aviator—bush pilot to you—it's the next explosive project scheduled by the PPP. Does the name mean anything to you?"

She frowned at me for a moment in the dim light. "Oh. You mean it's all come back to you? You *do* remember. . . . How come?"

"Easy," I said. "Next time you meet a poor amnesiac, just shoot the girl he's planning to marry, right through the heart. If you use another bullet to crease his cranium lightly, it helps. Everything will came back to him. I guarantee it."

Well, at least I could talk about it now. I no longer wanted to kill the whole world because of it. I guess it was a step in the right direction.

Sally Wong was staring at me in surprise. "You mean the Davidson? Were you actually planning to marry that cold snow maiden mourning chastely for her. . . . Oh, damn, I'm sorry, Paul. It just popped out. You know I didn't like her, but I didn't mean. . . ."

"Hush your mouth, Wong," I said. "The lady is dead, dead, dead."

"I said I was sorry."

I said maliciously, "You weren't such a hot snow maiden yourself, as I recall. I can't remember anything about you and me worth remembering, sweetheart, except several months of gentlemanly self-control, an exercise at which I do not normally excel. At least I don't like excelling at it. It was a hell of a frustrating mission all around for a virile gent like me, particularly since I'm not dimensioned for sleeping on people's living room sofas. That was where I seemed to get parked wherever I went, the past six months, with the frigid dame snoring peacefully in the next room."

"I don't snore," Sally said calmly, "and I'm not frigid, but. . . . well, you can't expect me to get serious about a man who just won't take my work seriously."

"Okay, and I can't be expected to get serious about a girl who takes my work too seriously."

She laughed. "Obviously, there's nothing wrong with your memory now, Paul. We're right back where we left off, fighting again."

"Make it Matt," I said, "That cover has served its purpose, and this is no place for a peaceful cameraman named Madden. Helm's the name, ma'am. And the subject is still Blossom. Operation Blossom." I tried to sit up. She helped me. I winced and said, "Oops, don't tip it or the brains will all run out through the crack. I think it's time for somebody to kick me in the tailbone for a change and give my poor headbone a rest."

It took me a moment to catch my breath from the effort and to let the throbbing pain subside. I could see her clearly now, kneeling beside me, small and pretty in her offbeat Chinese way—well, I don't suppose the Chinese consider it offbeat—but I was remembering that, as I'd indicated, we really hadn't got along too well in spite of the lovey-dovey act we'd put on in public as long as the mission required it. She'd had the attitude common to a lot of people with high moral principles; for the good of mankind they're sometimes willing to strangle their finer feelings and make reluctant use of a nasty specialist like me, but that doesn't mean they have to approve of him or respect his talents. And, on the other hand, I've never been able to appreciate the sublime arrogance of folks who feel they were put on earth just to save other folks from themselves, which seemed to be her main goal in life.

Fortunately for her, she was no longer wearing anything as expensive and vulnerable as the neat suit, blouse, and nylons in which she'd visited the hospital, it seemed a hell of a long time ago. She had on sturdy blue jeans and a blue quilted ski parka. Both were fairly well coated with greasy rust-brown goop from the walls and floors of our prison. In spite of her basically durable costume, she managed to project a bruised-flower image that reminded me painfully of another female I'd once liberated in moderately dilapidated condition—but of course this one wasn't liberated yet.

"Blossom," I said. "Concentrate on Blossom, Wong."

She thought a moment, and shook her head, "I'm sorry. It means absolutely nothing to me."

"How much time do you figure we've got for talking? How often do they check us?"

"There seems to be no set watch schedule," she said. "I've been in here since early last night. They grabbed me when I ran over to the grocery after work—I'm still marking time on that North-Air job, waiting for the final word on Walters. It was well after dark when we got here after about an hour and a half of driving. Every so often during the night somebody would shine a flashlight down, but the timing was completely irregular. I got the impression they consider themselves something of a para-military outfit, but the discipline leaves a lot to be desired. Around midnight, I guess it was, they lowered you down to me. They laughed when they told me I was getting company." She shivered. "At first I thought it was a horrible practical joke; I was sure you were dead. In the dark I couldn't even see who you were. I could just feel the blood. But the skull seemed to be intact, and then you moved a little and I could hear you breathing, but I had to wait until daylight before I could recognize.

142

. . . I haven't heard anybody out on deck for a couple of hours."

I hesitated. "What the hell do they want you for, anyway? Did they tell you?"

"Brace yourself," she said. "I'm wanted for crimes against the people. Somebody's apparently figured out that it wasn't just Herb Walters' manly charm that kept me at North-Air. I'm charged with luring said anti-establishment hero to his doom, meaning you. We'll both be brought to trial before a people's tribunal, properly constituted. Honest. That's what the woman said, with flourishes."

I said, wryly, "Looks like they're gaining confidence, and not just blowing up folks at random any longer. Now it's summary justice, PPP style; Kitty dead and you and I soon to be punished for our counter-revolutionary crimes. At least I suppose the firing squad comes right after the fair trial. Escape possibilities?"

Sally shook her head. "I don't think so. Not without a cutting torch or a great big wrench. It's a steel or iron hull, and there's a heavy partition back in the dark there. Some kind of an opening I could feel, but it's closed by a metal cover that's bolted on, and the bolts are very rusty. It would take a lot of leverage to budge them, if they can be budged. I've checked every inch of the place for some kind of a tool—that's how I got so filthy—but there's absolutely nothing. A big loading hatch above us, but it clamps from outside, just like the little manhole cover or whatever you call it. Otherwise it's just a big, empty iron coffin. Sorry."

I said, "You're pretty good, Wong. You make nice reports."

It took her by surprise. Then she said stiffly, "It's kind of you to concede, at last, that you're not the only one with adequate training around here, Mr. Helm."

I grinned. "Don't bite my head off, doll. But I guess it did sound kind of patronizing. From now on I'll stick to insults and let the compliments go, okay?"

She laughed quickly. "Tell me about Walters. Do you *know* that he's dead?"

"Yes, ma'am," I said. "He's dead, but it didn't work

out quite the way we planned it. The original idea, remember, approved by you and your superiors, was for me to get him to land on a fairly distant lake where I'd secretly cached some supplies on one of my previous bird watching expeditions. As soon as we were down, I'd dispose of him, sink the plane and body very deep—they've got some fairly bottomless ponds up there—and hike out. On the last day, of course, I'd ditch any supplies I had left and come crawling into civilization on hands and knees, a battered, emaciated survivor of a terrible wilderness crash, unable to say just what mountain it was we'd piled up against in the overcast. Very simple. With a bit of cooperation from the authorities, discreetly coached by your drug-busting superiors and their Canadian counterparts, it should have worked. Only Christofferson was wise. He knew I was after him. He didn't wait for us to land. Actually, I think it was that switch they had me make from one girl to another that had tipped him off about me; that wasn't really a very bright maneuver."

"What happened?"

"At least I was smart enough to see that he was getting ready for something," I said. "When he started easing his hand towards his gun, while we were still in the air, I showed him mine. He laughed at me. He pointed out that I didn't dare shoot him because I couldn't fly the plane. If I shot him, I'd crash and die. He was the chatty kind, when he had the upper hand. He wasn't in any hurry and he felt perfectly safe: he had it all figured out. He let me sit there holding my useless revolver while he told me how smart he was. Actually, not so smart. He had no idea he'd even been suspected of setting up a western drug operation for Brassaro. He assumed we'd been working on the terrorist angle right along. He said he knew what we were after, all right: information about the next blast, coming very soon. He said he'd give me a hint to take to hell with me, and he told me that name, Operation Blossom. Then he started reaching for his gun again, very slowly and deliberately, grinning at me, daring me to shoot him and leave myself high in the sky without a pilot, and with no place to go but down." I paused.

"The suspense is terrible," Sally said. "What did you do?"

I said, "Hell, I shot him, of course."

"But—"

"Mr. Walters hadn't done his homework. Those guys tend to sell themselves on their own bright ideas. They never make allowances for the possibility that they might be slightly wrong. If he'd done a little research in the right file—granted it isn't available in the public library, but some folks in Moscow have a reasonable facsimile, I believe, and maybe you could even find it in Peking—anyway, if he'd bothered to look in the right place he'd have learned that a certain U.S. agent, while he holds no license, once managed to put an aircraft down in a Mexican lagoon when the pilot suffered a sudden demise in midair. It didn't do the plane a damned bit of good, I'll admit, but the more important passengers, like me, escaped undamaged." I shrugged. "I figured that if I could do it in Mexico and survive, I could probably do it in Canada. At least it gave me a better chance than if I waited for him to put a slug through me."

"But you weren't found on that inland lake. How—"

"I was in too much of a hurry," I confessed. "Planes scare me. I was thinking too hard about what came next; about how I was going to get that damned bird downstairs in one piece. I didn't make sure of him first. He waited until I'd unfastened my belt, and then flipped the aircraft and threw me across the cabin, hard. By the time my head stopped spinning, not to mention the plane, he was really dead; but the lake for which we'd been heading wasn't there any more. There was nothing but clouds below with some nasty-looking mountains sticking up out of them. I tell you, Wong, for kicks just get yourself lost up in the air some time, in a plane with a limited gas supply that you don't really know how to fly. It's a *real* trip, baby; you can keep your damned LSD."

"Go on, Matt," she said softly.

"Well, I didn't dare go down into the soup and hunt for something wet to land on down among all those rocks

145

and trees," I said. "That Beaver is a *big* plane when you don't know what the hell you're doing; twice as big as the one I'd dunked down south. And those damned clumsy floats don't make it any easier to handle in close quarters. I just stayed up and headed west by compass looking for clear weather and a nice soft piece of ocean to crash down on before the gas gave out. I don't remember a hell of a lot about the flight; I don't suppose I ever will. I'd really taken a wallop, and I kept blacking out and coming back just in time to keep from flying into a cliff. Then I've got a picture of some big waves coming at me. The next thing I see clearly is the Prince Rupert Regional Hospital."

The girl beside me drew a long breath. "Maybe I don't entirely approve of what you do, even when you're doing it for us," she said after a moment, "but I've got to admit you seem to earn your money, whatever they pay you."

I said plaintively, "I keep telling people I'm a hero but they just won't listen. . . . Actually, it was a pretty poor performance and I deserved what I got." I frowned at her thoughtfully. "Hawaii," I said.

"What?"

"Before they sent me out here, they told me a little about the narcotics agent I'd be working with. You were born and raised in Hawaii, right?"

"Yes, but what in the world—"

"A *kanaka* by birth if not by blood," I said. "All Hawaiians swim like fish, isn't that correct?"

"Well, I'm a pretty good swimmer, Matt, but what—" She stopped and licked her lips. "I think I see what you mean. But do you know what the average survival time is in these waters at this time of year?"

I said, "Do you know what the average survival time is in a spot like this with people like this? If you see a chance, go. Don't try for the shore. The middle of the river; they won't be expecting you to head that way. Try to ride along with that current you told me about until you're clear, then fight your way ashore and find a phone. I'll do my best to cover for you if the break comes."

"But what about you—"

"Cut it out. That's amateur talk. You were just telling me what a well-trained pro you were. I fight better than you, if only because I'm bigger. You swim better than me. One of us has to get clear to pass the word about this place and you're the logical candidate. If you see a chance to go, go. And in order to have a better chance of getting that chance, if you follow me, remember that you were, are, and always have been an abject coward. I don't want to see the slightest vestige of pride or courage or self-respect, Miss Wong. You're a broken creature. A night in this horrible dirty black hole has cracked you wide open. Some tear-tracks down the face, please, some sniffles of fear, some choking hiccoughs of utter panic. Make it up as you go along, but make it good. Plead for your life if it seems indicated. Betray anything you're asked to betray including me. Whimper and whine. Maybe somebody will look away in utter disgust at being asked to guard such a piss-poor specimen of female humanity. That's when you go, okay?"

She didn't answer. She was listening. "I think they're coming," she said.

We heard the steel deck overhead reverberating with the impact of approaching footsteps. They were coming, all right. There wasn't time to make sure she'd really got what I was trying to tell her, or to confer about the finer details. There was only time for me, as senior officer present, to speak a few brave words of reassurance and encouragement.

"Hey, Wong," I said. "I—"

She interrupted in a singsong voice. "Me not Hey Wong, me Sally Wong. Hey Wong my uncle." She gave me a wink and a ghost of a smile. "Corny, huh? What were you going to say, Matt?"

"Never mind."

I'd never been much good at those going-into-action speeches anyway, and I had a distinct impression the troops here didn't really need one.

TWENTY

The hard part was getting up the ladder. I managed it with Sally pushing from below and a submachinegun beckoning from above. Like she'd said, straight magazine, skeleton stock. Even though I'd seen one once before, and even had my hands on it briefly, I still didn't recognize the weapon. Everybody's in the squirt-gun-production business these days, from north of the Finns to south of the Israelis. Well, if you want to be technical, there isn't much of anything north of the Finns, but you get the idea. You can't keep track of them all and there's no incentive. You don't find the class, workmanship, and individuality of, say, the old .45 Thompsons in these Johnny-come-lately mow-'em-down weapons. To a discriminating firearms fancier they're simply ingenious mechanical junk cobbled together from old gas pipes, coat hangers, and tin cans, of no esthetic value whatever, so who cares what name is crudely stamped on the receiver? Operationally, they're pretty much alike. They have to be so as not to confuse their users, the lazy and simple-minded gentry who can't be bothered with learning how to shoot so there's got to be something made available for routine homicide that can be sprayed like an aerosol can.

I did recognize the dark, broad face behind the weapon. It belonged to the guard who'd had the inside duty by the door when I arrived at the Inanook Sanitarium: a husky, square-built character. Later I'd seen him again. He'd been making the outside rounds one day as I was wheeled over to Elsie's Electrical Recreation Room by Tommy

148

Trask (poor Tommy) and I'd heard him called by name: Provost. Considering his security job it had seemed mildly amusing to me in my hazy, half-drugged condition— provost guard; guard Provost—so I remembered it now when I saw his face.

Emerging from the hatch I crouched there a moment, catching my breath. That got me a poke from the gun- barrel, urging me from my knees to my feet. Some men can never get hold of a weapon and somebody to point it at—well, women get the impulse, too, given the oppor- tunity—that they aren't overcome by an irresistible desire to use it as a cattle prod. It's been the death of some, but I wasn't up to trying anything fast and fancy at the moment; and there was a second man watching, similarly armed. Actually, I was happy just to discover, when I stood up, that the equilibrium gyros seemed to be func- tioning properly even though the main propulsive ma- chinery was way down on power. In other words, I seemed to be steady although weak. I was, of course, in utter agony from the pounding in my head, but we stoical undercover heroes learn to disregard such minor torments.

I was aware of Sally emerging from the hatch behind me, carefully covered by the weapon of the second man. It was the usual gray northwestern day with a moderate breeze. The brisk, damp air was reviving after the stale atmosphere of the hold; but as I stumbled weakly along the broad steel deck under Provost's urging, I managed to keep forward motion at a feeble minimum, giving myself time to check what I'd been told about our sur- roundings.

The brown, flooded river was there all right, sweeping past the sheltering little island—islet, rather—at a good clip, loaded with debris and driftwood. If she made it that far, she shouldn't have much trouble finding something to keep her afloat, as long as she had strength enough to hold onto it in that cold water. On the shoreward side, the pier against which we lay was higher than the barge by several feet. Apparently it had been constructed with even higher water levels in mind. It was L-shaped. We lay against the short outer end while the long stem of the L slanted up to the high granite shore. A gravel road ran down to it. In times past you could have driven out on it—it was plenty wide enough—but I wouldn't have wanted to try the splintered planks and ancient timbers now with anything much heavier than a bicycle.

The big question in my mind concerned the two boats she'd mentioned. Shuffling along slowly, I spotted them tied up to the rickety, floating small-craft dock beyond the barge. It was reached by the kind of hinged gangway that adjusts itself to the rise and fall of the tide, so apparently we were still in tidal waters.

The boats were as funny-looking as Sally had said: stubby, ugly little vessels. I'd learned enough about this northern lumber country in my photographic incarnation to know that they were designed specifically for capturing floating maverick logs, like the roaming maverick cattle that were the basis of so many trail herds back in the legendary days of the American West. I remembered that while researching the logging article I'd used to make plausible contact with Kitty Davidson, PR girl, I'd been told that the big lumber companies, like the cattle barons of old, frown upon these small independent operations based upon rounding up and selling unclaimed strays. However, the big boys can't seem to prevent some timber from escaping their endless booms and rafts, they aren't willing to spend money rounding up every errant log, and the drifting lumber is a serious menace to navigation. Consequently, the prowling independents with their small boats built specially for the purpose claim to be performing a public service, as well as making a living, and the public seems to agree at least to the extent of refraining from putting them out of business. The local maverick-lumber hunter had, I saw, a considerable gather of logs corralled in the nearby backwater.

As far as the boats were concerned, I was glad to see that one was an aging, motorless hulk, barely afloat. It wasn't going anywhere. The other had the cover of its big outboard motor removed. Transparent plastic had been taped around the powerhead to protect it while an essential part was being repaired. Okay. If Sally could make it into the water, nobody'd be chasing her under power. All they could do was shoot at her if they felt secure enough in this quiet cove to make that much noise; and a duck on the water is a poor target and a human in the water is worse. At least it was nice to think so.

Provost gave me another poke to hurry me along. It didn't bother me greatly. I felt no strong resentment. I realized that I was actually in a rather strange mental condition. Remote, I guess is the word. Whether it was caused by the return of my memory or by the bullet bouncing off my skull, I didn't quite seem to be there. I could chatter brightly about the past and present, I could make notes about my surroundings in endless detail —maybe too endless detail—but it all seemed to concern somebody else, not me. It was a little like the deliberate withdrawal I'd employed at Inanook when things got rough.

I heard Sally whimper convincingly with pain and fear as her escort, whom I didn't recognize, also used his gun muzzle for stimulation purposes. Out here in full daylight, she was a pitiful sight indeed, with her frightened, streaked little face and her rust-smeared clothes. I was a fairly pitiful sight myself, I realized as I approached the deckhouse with its reflecting glass: my face, shirt, and jacket were heavily caked with dried blood from the crease in my scalp. The reddish muck from the barge interior improved the effect. I looked as if I'd been exhumed from a damp grave. Great. The worse we looked, the better chance we had of being usefully underestimated.

But the glimmer of optimism, if that was what it had been, died abruptly as we were shoved inside. I'd assumed that the next act of the play would be performed in the cabin at deck level, giving Sally a reasonable shot at the door if I could manage a suitable diversion. Instead, once inside what seemed to be a small ship's galley complete with stove, sink, and refrigerator—an open door gave me a glimpse of a shabby bunkroom aft—we were shown another open hatch and a ladder leading back down into the bowels of the barge.

"I'll cover them, Manny," said Provost. "You get down there and yell when you're ready for them."

We stood quite still under Provost's gun while Manny,

a small, wiry individual with a weak, whiskery chin, stepped to the edge of the hatch. He laid his machine pistol carefully on the steel decking, lowered himself into the hole, took the weapon and passed it to somebody below, and disappeared from sight. In a moment his voice reached us.

"Ready here. Jake says send the man down first."

Provost gestured with his chopper. I moved forward, turned my back to the hatch as Manny had done, got to my knees, and groped with one foot for the first rung of the ladder below me. I didn't look at Sally. She'd seemed bright and alert enough not to need any betraying signals. It would have to be a semi-sacrifice play, of course. Once down there, we didn't stand a chance of escape, either of us. From up here, one of us might get clear to carry the message to Garcia, the sad word from Thermopylae, the good news from Ghent to Aix, wherever they might be—I'd read the poem as a kid but I'd never checked out the geography.

I kept feeling around clumsily with my foot, clinging to the edge of the hole in the floor, hoping that Provost, impatient, would take just one step closer so I could dump him on his can and give the girl her break. I hoped she'd have sense enough to blast off without looking back. There's be nothing for her to see except Heroic Helm getting pleasantly massacred by automatic firearms below and above—that is, unless he managed to roll clear of the one and grab the other, not really a very promising undertaking. Provost's foot moved. . . .

"Please be careful, Mr. Helm."

It was a new voice—well, new for today. I'd heard it before, however. I looked towards the bunkroom door, and there he was, the little round man who, gowned and masked and capped like a surgeon, had watched all the fun and games in Elsie's back room: Heinrich Glock, alias Heinie the Clock, alias John Ovid. He had a pump-action shotgun resting in the crook of his arm and I hadn't really expected him to use anything else, except when he was on rifle duty of course. The doublebarreled jobs give you only two shots. The autoloaders tend to be temperamental. A pump will shoot as fast as an auto in expert hands—some say faster—and it practically never jams. Twelve gauge. Number One Buck. Within, say, forty yards, certain death. You can go up against a chopper with some faint hope, but there's no real hope against a scattergun, sixteen pellets to the load.

I studied him for a moment. He was a dapper figure in a dark overcoat and a narrow-brimmed hat that made his white moon face look even rounder than it was, an effect emphasized by the round, gold-rimmed glasses. Just an owly-looking little fellow in neat city clothes and polished city shoes holding a great big shotgun—ridiculous. Well, ridiculous if you didn't look too closely at the sharp, cold eyes behind the book-keeper glasses. Of course I wasn't really seeing him clearly. Instead I was seeing a girl lying dead in a fragile pink gown stained with dark red blood.

I told myself that was entirely beside the point; I was allowing myself to be distracted by purely personal considerations of no significance here. Hatred didn't count, I informed myself firmly; revenge was irrelevant. He was just another man with a gun who had to be put out of business with the rest of this blast-happy crew, preferably before they could indulge in any more fatal fireworks. It wasn't the job for which I'd been sent to this part of the continent, that was all taken care of, but if these terrorist creeps had the poor judgement to interfere with my plans for living I'd damned well show them some great plans for dying. . . . Cut it out, Agent Eric. Snap out of it! What the hell do you think you are, anyway, some kind of avenging angel with a shining sword?

But it had broken through the remoteness: a sudden, white-hot blast of rage like the one that had set me to playing Horatius at the Bridge with kitchen knives back in Kitty's apartment. Stupid. Forget the pretty lady in pink. Mourn her on your own time. Right now, just pull your scrambled brains together and figure a way to get your Hawaiian fish-girl of Chinese descent past that twelve-bore blunderbuss. . . . But there was no way. I knew she'd never make it now, even if I did manage to escape Manny's gun, below, and disarm Provost, above. I'd never make it, either. The little man with the pumpgun would make a neat double, bang-clackety-bang, like dropping a pair of crossing ducks, and that would be the end of that.

I looked at him and saw that, relaxed as he looked, he was ready. He didn't even have to shoulder the weapon at this range although, being a careful workman, he probably would. He turned his head slightly and the window-reflections off his glasses turned his face into a blind round mask. His prim little mouth spoke.

"I regret that the death of the Davidson woman was considered necessary, Mr. Helm," he said calmly. "But we are both professionals, *hein?* We know what it is to follow orders. Now please go below. You can see that resistance is foolish."

Sally Wong glanced at him, a little puzzled by his attitude. I was a little puzzled myself, but there was no time to figure out exactly what had puzzled me. Provost had sensed something wrong and stepped back out of reach.

He said harshly, "Stop stalling, you, and get the hell down there before I kick you down."

I found the rung in the right place that I'd been searching for in the wrong place. With both feet supported, I looked down. Manny's ratty little figure awaited me below. What I could see of the chamber in which he stood reminded me of hunting cabins I'd known a long time ago, crowded with men and firearms, dim with tobacco smoke —although, from the aroma, these combustion products did not all originate as tobacco.

"What the shit is going on here?" Still another new voice for today, this one feminine. My head and shoulders were still above the galley floor. I looked up and saw a woman in a long skirt standing in the doorway, silhouetted against the outside light. "What the fuck are the prisoners doing out, Provost?" she demanded. "I said to keep them locked up until we had time to deal with them properly. Jeez, a girl can't step out of the fucking house to plant a little dynamite without a bunch of jerks getting crappy ideas while she's gone!"

154

It had taken a long time, but I had a hunch I was finally making the acquaintance of the mysterious Mrs. Market.

TWENTY-ONE

It took them a while to sort it out. I remained carefully motionless on the ladder until I got clearance from all parties concerned, above and below. I didn't want either my head or my tail shot off by somebody with a machine pistol who felt I was moving the wrong way. Then I eased myself cautiously back up into the barge's cabin and got to my feet.

The remote feeling had come back. I knew I was missing something, and it concerned Ovid, but I couldn't dredge it up. In the meantime I wasn't really listening to the woman who now knelt by the hatch I'd just vacated, yelling obscenities downward, or to the man who was answering from the interior of the barge with equally violent but somewhat less colorful language. I recognized his voice. He was the one who wanted to finish me off in Kitty's apartment but a woman, this woman, had stopped him. As before I knew I'd heard his voice elsewhere but I couldn't make the connection. I made note of the fact that there seemed to be a policy difference involved that went beyond the mere disposition of a couple of prisoners. However, the squabble didn't seem important enough to justify a major effort of concentration.

The important fact was that they were squabbling and the dissension might yield an opening sooner or later. In the meantime there was nothing much to be accomplished with Ovid on guard and Provost alerted. After a little, I caught the ex-security-man's eye and gestured towards the galley sink, making cautious face-washing motions. He started to shake his head, but Ovid said something I couldn't hear for the yelling. Provost hesitated, shrugged, and made a small motion with the submachinegun to indicate that it was okay for me to proceed in the desired direction, but I'd hardly started to move when he stopped me again. He sidled past and reached for something in the shadows at the end of the counter, a long, plastic guncase that I hadn't spotted, leaning there. It had the bulky look of a case designed for a rifle with a telescopic sight, so I knew what gun it was and what it had been used for. He made his cautious way past me once more and handed the cased rifle to Ovid, who set it in a corner out of reach with a tolerant smile, knowing, as did I, that the idea of my being able to get the gun free and load it in time to tackle two armed men with ready weapons was faintly ridiculous.

Provost gave me the okay signal with his expressive gunbarrel. I stepped over there and found a big black rubber plug that looked as if it had been used as a teething ring by a carnivorous baby. I stuck it into the drain. There was only one faucet. It spat cold water reluctantly when I turned it on. I speculated about where the wet stuff was coming from since this wasn't a fancy marina with hose connections, but I guess that's one of the things I'll never know.

They were still arguing hotly. You could call it good news and bad news. I mean, a well organized, united, disciplined enemy is certainly harder to defeat in theory; but in practice you never know when some hothead in a bunch of quarreling, disorganized screwballs is going to blow you away by mistake. I peeled a paper towel from a tattered roll, dampened it, and started to mop at my face.

"Here, let me." Sally Wong took the wad of paper, now pink with watery blood, from my fingers. Then she stopped, as if overcome by her fears. "M-Matt what are they going to do to us?" she wailed. "What's going to happen to us?"

"Keep your chin up, sweetheart," I said.

"You damned fool," she said in a lower voice.

"What did I do?"

"They'd have got you for sure if you'd tried it. Even without that little man and his shotgun."

I said, "So I die at the top of a ladder instead of the bottom. Big deal." More loudly, I snapped, "For Christ's sake stop wetting your pants like a baby, you're a big girl now. How the hell did a washout like you ever get into this racket in the first place?"

"I d-didn't know it would be like this! I thought it was going to be exciting and glamorous . . . glamorous! Look at me, I've never been so dirty in my life!"

Provost stirred irritably. "Shut up! No talking!"

Sally sniffed loudly, gulped, and turned to the job at hand. I stood still while she removed the worst of the clotted gore. I saw that another woman was standing silent in the doorway, a short, stout girl in enormous, grimy, baggy jeans and a man's wool shirt, worn with the tails out. She had a man's felt hat on her stringy brown hair. She leaned against the doorjamb totally without expression. I had the feeling she's stand there forever, looking blank, until somebody told her to stand somewhere else. It was really a hell of a grubby operation, I reflected wryly. No class at all. Next time I'd ask to be assigned to the Casino at Monte Carlo, in full evening dress under crystal chandeliers, accompanied by a gorgeous creature in shimmering satin carrying a pearl-handled pistol in her diamond-studded evening bag. Next time.

Sally was working around the bullet-cut in my scalp, cautiously, when the screaming match stopped. Joan Market rose, settled her coarse wool serape about her shoulders, and came over. She shoved Sally aside.

"Never mind that, we don't care how fucking pretty he looks," she snapped. She turned her attention to me, studied me for a moment, and said, "So this is the great assassinator, sudden death on wheels. How many fucking people have you killed, really?"

I took a chance. I didn't want to go too far in antagonizing her since she seemed to be, for the moment, on our side in some peculiar way—at least she wasn't howling for an instant kill. On the other hand, I was supposed to be the brave, strong prisoner here, facing death courageously to draw attention from my frightened, insignificant little oriental colleague.

I said, "If I'm supposed to take that question literally, the answer is none."

Her eyes narrowed. "What's the point of lying about it? Hell, I myself know of four, maybe five, and one more who probably won't survive that goddamned butcher knife you flipped into his chest. . . ." She stopped and let out a sharp bray of laughter. "Oh. I see. Literally, huh? You mean when you killed them they weren't. . . . Funny!"

She was a moderately tall young woman who was heavier than she needed to be. She gave the impression that, just as her foul language was undoubtedly a reaction against the way she'd been brought up—I would have bet on a college degree—so the sloppy extra weight was a deliberate response to all the sexist advertising instructing the female of the human species to be slim and clean and attractive to the male. She was also, of course, rebelling against the old reactionary cult of cleanliness. They all do that, all the real blue-denim kids. Well, hell, I'm not totally sold on mouthwashes and anti-perspirants myself. I've spent considerable time with unwashed gentlemen in situations involving limited sanitation facilities and heavy stress; an unwashed lady doesn't shock me tremendously, or at least no more than one who makes a religion of being totally immaculate, dry, deodorized and untouchable. I mean, there's got to be a happy medium somewhere.

Actually, she wasn't a bad-looking girl. My first thought was that she had some black ancestors; then I decided that, although it was a full-lipped, blunt-nosed face, the Negroid effect was largely due to the wild, fuzzy, phony-African hairdo. Her eyes scared me because, in contrast with the crazy hair, they weren't crazy at all. They were brown eyes, calm and intelligent. They reminded me a little of the brown eyes of Dr. Elsie Somerset that, aside from a faint glow of pleasure, had never displayed any real madness even when the woman was cranking up her rheostat to the higher numbers on the dial.

Joan Market stared at me searchingly a moment longer, then turned her head and said, "Ruthie, go get the little monsters ready, no, tell somebody to do it, huh? And then come into the council room, you're a member and we've got to hold a meeting, a fucking *meeting*, for God's sake! Today, for God's sake! Everybody's losing their idiot marbles around here. Well, go *on*!"

"Yes, Joanie."

It took the fat girl a while to make the response and move towards the hatch, as if all the processes were sluggish, both mental and physical.

"Yes, Joanie!" said Joan Market in a soft, sour voice as Ruthie made her way through the hatch with some difficulty. "Shit. Morons and maniacs, that's what we've got, morons and maniacs." She turned back to look at me once more. "You. You kill people so is there any reason people shouldn't kill you?"

"Not any," I said. "If they can manage."

"We'll manage," she said. "You bet we'll fucking manage. We'll wipe you out and everything you represent, all the oppression and injustice backed by establishment guns in the hands of men like you."

"Is an establishment gun any worse than an anti-establishment gun?" I jerked my head towards the submachinegun in Provost's hands.

"Shit," she said, "I didn't want us to get into that firearms bit at all, we were doing fine without it. Only General Jacques Frechette of the People's Army of Liberation of the People's Protest Party, that great champion of the poor and downtrodden, he had to have the fucking toys for his fucking boys. The People's Army of Liberation, all nine of them or is it eleven? All colonels and majors and lieutenants, not a private in the bunch. What's your rank, Provost?"

"Major, ma'am."

"Major Provost Littlebird, PAL, PPP. Oh, my God! Sorry, Vostie, you're okay, it's just the idea that makes me want to puke. We had a good thing going, we were getting somewhere, we had the arrogant establishment bastards almost softened up enough to listen to our demands, and then we had to start playing idiot, little-boy war games, guerilla games, for God's sake. . . . What the hell is everybody waiting for, anyway? If we're going to have a meeting let's *have* the fucking meeting. *Frechette*."

Somebody yelled from below, "Keep your pants on, Joanie!"

"What pants?" she asked of nobody in particular. She frowned at Sally and me. "Don't get any crazy idea that I'm your friend, either of you. It's just such a goddamned *waste*. A man like you, Helm, a typical establishment mercenary, you and your sexy little accomplice, Shanghai Sally here, Jesus, we could have made you into important symbols of exactly the ruthless and unscrupulous repressive methods we're fighting against if everybody wasn't in such a goddamned rush. A trial before a real people's tribunal, not a hole-and-corner lynching on this shitty little floating shithouse. And today, for God's sake? Why the hell today?"

"What's so special about today?" I asked, gambling. "Could it have anything to do with Operation Blossom, by any chance?"

Her eyes narrowed. She stared into my face. "You were supposed to have lost your memory," she said softly. "It came back?"

"It never went away," I said. "We figured, if I pretended to forget everything Walters had told me, you bomb-freaks might feel safe enough to go ahead with it and let us catch you in the act—"

Her laughter stopped me. "Nice try," she said. "Now we're supposed to call it off thinking the fuzz knows all about it? Clever, but there are two things wrong, Helm. The first is that Elsie Somerset was a damned good head doctor, and if she said you had amnesia, amnesia is what you had. She couldn't break through it, but it was there. Then. And while you may have since remembered something you heard from Walters—I guess you have or you wouldn't know about Blossom—it either wasn't very much or you haven't got the word to anybody who matters. Because you see I just planted that boom-boom device a couple of hours ago, and nobody paid me a bit of attention, and I've done enough of them now that I'd *know* if there was a trap. Now get the hell back there

161

so we can get this over and concentrate on something important. . . . You, too, you sniveling little Mata Hari. Move!"

TWENTY-TWO

To build the cabin they'd fastened beat-up six-by-sixes, that had once been used for something else, to the barge's rusty steel decking and worked up from there. It was not a nautical structure but strictly a do-it-yourself project as Sally had said. Real ship's carpentry is different, carefully fitted, solidly assembled with wood screws and bolts. This was just a floating shack put together from secondhand lumber by people who didn't know how to drive nails straight and didn't care. There were mismatched window frames and illfitting doors.

From the galley we were taken into what I'd thought to be a large communal bedroom because I'd glimpsed a couple of untidy cots through the open door. I'd thought wrong. It turned out to be a mess hall of sorts, with a homemade table—just boards on trestles—and an assortment of crippled chairs. A wood stove in the far corner threw out a considerable amount of heat that felt very good after the chill of our recent prison. The place was littered with dirty clothes and other debris. The cots I'd seen had apparently just been stuck back in the corner to handle the overflow from the real bunkroom beyond, visible through the door at the end of the room. It seemed to be a smaller chamber with doubledeckers along the wall. I couldn't determine how they solved the bathroom problem. Certain stale odors hinted that whatever the solution was, it wasn't perfect.

But there were only two details of the construction and layout that really concerned me. The fact that the shanty was made of wood, instead of mild shipbuilding steel like the barge itself, meant that it wouldn't begin to stop bullets, not even bullets from the fairly feeble pistol ammo I figured was used in the local variety of automatic firearms. At least it was a good bet that the caliber was 9mm Parabellum—Luger to you—since most of them, at least those of non-communist origin, take that cartridge these days and the hole in the business end of Provost's weapon looked about right. The flimsy siding couldn't even be counted on to stop buckshot, although those little round lead balls don't penetrate much. Our escape strategy would have to allow for this. It wouldn't be enough just to whip around a corner out of sight. Either chopper or shotgun could make any position untenable out there if the operator was willing to make a lot of noise and rip up the shack a bit.

On the plus side of the ledger was the fact that the way we'd entered, through the galley, wasn't the only way to get into the dining room, if you want to call it that—or out of it. There was another door leading directly out onto the barge's seaward deck from the far end of the room. Of course, until we got a good close look at it, or until somebody used it, we couldn't know if it was readily operable. It might be locked or simply nailed shut.

I tried not to give it more than a casual look as Provost shepherded us down the shoreward side of the room past the long table, to the nearest cot. He told us to sit down and behave ourselves, or words to that effect. As he moved on by, cautiously, I was aware of Sally casting a quick glance across the room to measure the distance she'd have to go; by the time Provost had taken up station in the bunkroom doorway, she'd buried her face in my left shoulder, sniffling hopelessly. Ovid had remained at the door by which we'd come.

A couple of small kids in ragged jeans and T-shirts, hair long, sex undeterminable, were playing some kind of game at the table. They didn't seem particularly intrigued by the sight of prisoners and firearms. Joan Market, who'd followed us in, went over and told them to beat it, there was going to be a meeting of the council. They said aw-nuts-do-we-have-to and shuffled out through the door facing us, leaving it ajar. Okay. I heard Sally draw a long, controlled breath beside me and let it out again. Joan Market marched over and slammed the door shut; she had to kick it to make it latch. I heard the kids race by outside, making plenty of noise on the reverberating deck. Then the voice of the fat girl, Ruthie, called from the galley, and they charged in there and clattered down the ladder into the barge's interior.

Although there had been a reference to little monsters earlier, I'd been mildly shocked at the actual sight of children, but they were obviously an essential part of the camouflage. Take some grubby hippie families—or whatever the dropout term is nowadays—living together on a funny-looking shanty boat complete with grubby kids, and nobody'd bother to keep track of how many different men were seen coming and going, or women either. Everybody knows that the personnel of those sinful groups is forever changing in a most promiscuous way. Unless you were firmly dedicated to bringing soap, haircuts, and morals to everybody, or taking drugs away from them, you'd pay very little attention to this raggedy backwoods commune once it became clear that the members minded their own business and didn't bother anybody or steal anything. Sooner or later questions might be asked about sanitation or education, but with care the hideout could probably operate unsuspected for a considerable time.

I didn't think it would operate much longer, whatever happened. It had obviously been the secret headquarters from which instructions had been sent to the more conspicuous installation at Inanook; but they could hardly expect to remain safe here now that they were organizing terrorist incidents in their own back yard. The Tsawwassen ferry explosion had been bad enough from a security standpoint; another blast here in the Vancouver area would raise a local manhunt that would overlook nothing, certainly not an unconventional setup like this. They must have plans for getting out fast and setting up shop elsewhere. . . .

"That bomb," Sally breathed between muffled sobs. "The one that woman just planted. It can't be too far away. Somewhere in the city, probably. We've got to find out where and when. We've got to stop it."

"Not we," I whispered. "Your job is to get clear and bring the cavalry here. Concentrate, Wong. Don't get distracted by a little bit of dynamite, or nitro, or TNT. Straight out that door and over the side the instant you see a break. Remember, the first couple of steps are what will count when that table is full of people. Once you're behind them, they'll shield you from Ovid, and even Provost can't cut loose without mowing down half of them, not until you're past him and grabbing for the doorknob. I'll try to keep him out of action long enough. . . ." I shoved her away irritably. "For Christ's sake stop sniffling on me, you're driving me nuts!"

Mrs. Market paced by without a glance at us, her long denim skirt swinging, frayed around the bottom to a whitish fringe. I wondered idly how a hem had got to be considered a reactionary political institution, to be rejected by all liberated spirits. It's always seemed to me a very sensible way of finishing off a garment, which undoubtedly betrays my basic fascistic tendencies. I couldn't help noting that, hemmed or frayed, light or heavy, the lady had a smooth, springy, predatory way of moving, like a large, caged cat. She paused at the galley door where Ovid played sentry. He stepped aside, thinking she meant to pass, but she turned abruptly and squeezed past the chair at the head of the rustic table to the window there. She stood looking out at the brown river, drumming her fingers nervously against the rain-streaked glass.

Okay. Recheck. Exit door straight ahead across the room. Provost in the bunkroom doorway close and to the left—maybe there was another escape route through there he wanted to block. Ovid in the galley doorway at the other end of the room, far and to the right. As long as we remained still they had us in a safe crossfire without a worry about shooting the people at the table or each other. However, if we moved, assuming we could move fast enough or one of us could. . . .

Ovid stepped aside once more and Ruthie came in and said something to Joan Market. The taller woman, still watching the sullen river, waved her away with a sharp don't-bother-me gesture. Ruthie sat down on the far side of the table, placidly undisturbed; apparently rejection was her normal lot in life and she expected nothing else. Soon the rest of them were filing in, another woman in a long, oldfashioned dress, followed by three men. The woman was young, with a pinched small face and a lot of dark, stringy hair, kept under some kind of control by a red band around her head. Then came little Manny, whom we'd already met, complete with chopper, followed by a husky young black man with a moderate Afro and dirty military-type coveralls. They split up. Manny and Redband took our side of the table. Coveralls went around to sit beside Ruthie, who gave him a shy little smile of greeting that made her face look quite pretty for a brief instant.

He'd obviously waited to make his entrance, General Jacques Frechette of the People's Protest Party, sometimes referred to as Jake. I'd made the connection by this time, of course. Watching him march in, I remembered that the last time I'd seen him he'd been wearing a scared look and an Inanook security-guard uniform with an empty holster. I remembered that he'd been very, very slow reaching for the revolver that had been in the holster. Perhaps for this reason, he was now carrying a submachinegun, which he laid at the head of the table ceremoniously, as if it were a symbol of office like a gavel.

Today he was wearing clean blue jeans and a short, matching denim jacket. On his lean frame, the outfit had a sharp, almost military, look; you half-expected to see a display of campaign ribbons over the pocket of the jacket. His old-frontiersman face was as picturesque as ever, with its drooping moustache and fierce eyebrows. His pale blue eyes swept the room in a commanding manner until they reached me. I saw him, momentarily disconcerted, remember how I'd disarmed and bullied him in Elsie Somerset's office. After a moment he showed me a look of malicious triumph: it was his turn now. He pulled back his chair, and paused, and glanced at the woman still standing by the window.

"If Mrs. Market is quite ready, we can call the meeting to order," he said briskly, and sat down without waiting for her, and went on, "You'll be glad to hear that the traitor Davidson—traitress, rather—has paid with her life for her treachery and deceit, setting an example I hope will be taken to heart by others who entertain foolish notions of joining our ranks under false pretenses." He stopped as Joan Market seated herself beside him, waited pointedly until she was still, and then continued: "I'm also happy to report that a well-executed raid by the People's Army of Liberation has netted two prisoners involved in the same establishment plot to penetrate our organization. We are faced with the problem of determining punishment suitable for this crime against the people. Speaking for myself, I'll state that I feel the male prisoner deserves no consideration from us. He comes with bloody hands to this room, and the blood is that of our comrades."

There was a little murmur of anger, as Frechette paused dramatically. I remembered that he'd had a phony-Frenchy accent at Inanook. Apparently it had been a disguise; he certainly didn't have it now.

"The case of the female prisoner is a little less clearcut, but only a little," he went on. "But before we take up the question of her guilt, let us review the great popular movement we represent, and remind ourselves of what is at stake here that transcends all considerations of sentiment and bourgeois humanitarianism. . . ."

Then he was off. It was quite a speech. He went back to the death of the tyrant Caesar at the hands of that great people's liberator, Brutus, and took it from there. We heard about the IRA, the PLO, FLQ, the SLA, and numerous other initials that meant nothing to me. The Weathermen and the Muslims each got a patronizing pat on the head along with protest movements I'd never heard of on continents I'd never visited and was fairly sure he hadn't, either. We got Bolívar and Juarez, Guevara and Arafat. . . .

There was a crash as Joan Market struck the flimsy table with both fists, rising. The room was suddenly silent.

"What are you trying to do to me?" she whispered. *"What are you trying to do to me?"*

TWENTY-THREE

I felt the barge shift positions minutely against the dock in response to wind or current. I could hear the faint sound of a radio or TV set operating down in the hold under my feet, and I wondered how much reception they could get surrounded by all that metal. I wondered absently what kind of a miserable, dank, dark metal cave of a dormitory they had down there. The above-deck accommodations were bad enough. Frechette stirred in an embarrassed way and looked up at the woman standing tall above him with her wild hairdo making her look even taller.

"Now, Joanie," he said mildly.

"You left out Jesus Christ and George Washington," she sneered. "Don't give me that now-Joanie shit! You know what today is. You know what I have to do today. What the hell do you think I am? Making me sit here and listen to this crap when you know I've got to make myself *right* about it before I do it, killing people isn't just a natural function like going to the can!"

He cleared his throat. "Certain decisions must be made—"

"They don't must be made today! I asked you to put it off; what's the goddamned rush? Corny speeches don't must be made today and I don't must listen to a lot of bullshit before I. . . . Damn you, Jake, what is it with you these days, anyway? We had it all settled a long time ago, you and Danny and I. We were going to have a *real* revolutionary movement, not just another goddamned yak-yak group-therapy outfit. No goddamned wild-eyed speeches. No Goddamned military titles. No crappy secret-agent code names. No goddamned secret guerilla armies or delusions of grandeur, no corny secret headquarters where we could be trapped, just a small bunch of dedicated underground fighters moving fast, moving silently, striking where it would hurt the bastards worst—and it was working, damn you, it was *working*! We had them running scared, by God. And now look at us, blasted out of that fucking crazy-house hideout, penned up in this weirdo floating pigsty! Who the hell needs a headquarters, anyway? Who needs all that rat-tat-tat guns? What's it all for except a goddamned ego trip—"

Frechette said stiffly, "It has been clearly demonstrated that an organization like ours must have efficient administration and strong defensive capabilities."

"Defensive bullshit!" she said. "We don't defend, we attack. And we were attacking damned successfully until you—"

"Were we?" he snapped, interrupting her. His voice was sharp. "Well, I suppose you're right up to a point, my dear. We *were* attacking successfully until your husband Danny blew himself up with one of his homemade bombs, a martyr to the Cause or to his own clumsiness, I've never quite figured out which!"

She had swung to face him. "Don't you sneer at Danny! Don't you *dare* sneer at Danny!"

"My apologies. I forgot. Dan Market bungled a simple job so he is now one of the brightest saints of our movement. Of course, I'll admit he did manage to take the Davidson girl's weakling husband with him, let's give him credit for that. Even if he did it by accident instead of according to our prearranged plan, he silenced *that* traitor in time, which is more than can be said for the way his wife was handled. I told you she wasn't to be trusted, remember? I told you she suspected the truth, she had to suspect the truth about how her husband died and why. I told you it was all just a trick—"

"And then you said we should let the bitch in anyway so we could keep an eye on her, remember?"

"Mr. Chairman!" It was the young black man in the green coveralls. "Mr. Chairman, General, sir, can we please get back to the subject of the meeting and skip the recriminations, sir?" His voice wasn't nearly as respectful as his words.

"Point well taken," Frechette said after a moment's pause. "You hear the man, Joanie. The subject is—"

"I know what the subject is," Joan Market snapped. "The real subject is one of the fancy remote-controlled explosive fucking devices we're using these days. It was planted this morning by Ruthie and me. It's now going to have to be fired on schedule by somebody. Who wants the job? Here!"

The cabin was silent once more as she dug into one of the big pockets of her skirt and brought out a black plastic object that seemed to be a diminutive transistor radio. She laid it on the table and flicked a switch with her thumb. I heard the girl with the red headband, closest to me, suck in her breath sharply as a tiny red light appeared in a corner of the plastic case.

"It's really very simple," Joan Market said. "Just turn it on like a radio, remember? You can even get AM programs on it, so keep the volume all the way down when the time comes unless you want to do it to a country-and-western accompaniment. Or the goddamned news. It *is* a radio and nobody can tell different without taking it apart. But if you're in the right area, anywhere within a quarter of a mile, and press the button—here—that says DIAL LIGHT, it will come in louder than any radio you ever heard. It will sound like the end of the world, and that's just what it will be for a lot of people. Since you've made it clear you don't want to leave me in peace to do it my way, there it is. All yours, General Frechette."

She pushed it towards him. He didn't move to take it. She made an angry sound in her throat.

"What's the matter, General Jake?" she demanded. "Here's your chance to do it your way. Ruthie'll brief you. She'll show you where to wait, where you'll be safe from the blast but close enough, and she'll handle the kids for camouflage—see that dirty hippie family wouldn't you think they'd take a bath sometimes—and get them the hell out of the area before it's time. Robbie's very good about having to go pee on cue, and Sissy likes spraying the paint around. And Ruthie'll tell you the signal you'll be given by a sanctified messenger of that great friend of humanity and social reform, Mr. Emilio Brassaro." The woman started to turn away, and glanced back. "Oh, you'd better switch it off now or you'll run down the batteries. Good luck, General."

Frechette reached out and caught her arm. "Where are you going?"

"Anywhere!" she said harshly. "Any fucking where away from this bunch of phony playacting revolutionaries. Come see the boys and girls in that great dramatic masterpiece Frechette's Last Stand. Rat-tat-tat, ratatatat, boom, bang. I should have split long ago. I should have split the day we got tied up with that crummy New York gangster and his coldeyed gunmen, and I do mean you Mr. Ovid or whatever the hell your real name is. We should have told the bastard to go fuck himself right at the start."

"You talk as if we had a choice!" Frechette protested. "You know there was no choice, Joanie. With Danny dead we had no way of getting the explosives we needed and nobody who knew how to construct. . . . Anyway, Brassaro had us cold. He'd have tipped off the authorities if we hadn't agreed to cooperate."

"So we took his tricky bombs, and his shitty secondhand machineguns, and used the Grade B movie sets he fixed up for us to hide in—"

"Mr. Brassaro has been very helpful, and our weapons and hideouts were provided at my request and to my specifications. I'll have you know I have given a great deal of thought to our needs, Joanie, and while I don't expect gratitude I think you could at least refrain from criticizing other people's administrative efforts until you've faced a few of the problems yourself."

The woman jerked herself free. "I know. All I do is make the stuff go bang while you march around at the head of your ten-man army. Well, *you* try pushing the bang-button for a change and see what it's like. Face that problem for a change. Even if I wasn't sick of listening to you, I'm tired of trying to kid myself that we can struggle for human freedom and dignity and deal with a parasite like Brassaro at the same time."

I glanced towards the little man with the shotgun, but he seemed unmoved by the reference to his current employer. Frechette threw him an uneasy glance, also.

"Maybe Mr. Brassaro's motives aren't as pure as we'd like them to be," he said stiffly, "but he is fighting the same establishment enemy that we face. To that extent he is a logical ally, and if we're too delicate to use help that's offered us. . . ."

"You sound as if it were handed out free of charge."

"We fulfill certain conditions," Frechette said with a show of patience. "We're told the time and place and signal instead of operating at random as we did when Danny was alive. Is that so important? The psychological effect on our enemies is the same, isn't it? We're still softening them up for the day we present our demands. In return for weapons to defend ourselves with, suitable places to hide from their Gestapo, and bombs that fire when they're supposed to instead of blowing us up by mistake, we sacrifice only a small freedom of choice."

The woman made a sharp gesture. "Well, I'm taking what freedom of choice I've got left and getting to hell out of here. And I still say you'd better turn that thing off before the batteries go dead on you." She watched Frechette's hand go out towards the radio and stop. She laughed shrilly. "What's the matter? The stuff is miles away. Are you scared of a little bitty crummy radio?" She reached out and pushed the switch, extinguishing the pinpoint of red light. She looked down the table towards Sally and me, but her eyes seemed to be focused far beyond us. Without looking down, she spoke to Frechette: "You'd louse it up, wouldn't you, Jake? After all the trouble we've had setting this one up, you'd go in there and try to fire at the wrong time or from the wrong distance, anything to make it easy and safe. If there's a way to fuck it up, you'll fuck it. Because you're bombshy, aren't you, Jake? That time Danny's bomb went off too soon and almost got you, too. You've been scared of them ever since, haven't you?"

The man surprised me. Instead of becoming indignant, he said quite gently, "I'll happily admit that, Joanie, if

173

you'll reconsider. You know we all have tremendous faith in you. We need you."

It sounded a little phony and overdone to me, but the woman thought about it quite seriously, frowning. When she spoke, her voice had changed oddly, becoming higher, almost childlike.

"You haven't left me much time."

"You have several hours yet, dear," said Frechette.

"You don't know what I go through," Joan Market said plaintively in that soft, high, new voice. "You never seem to understand that I mustn't be distracted on these special days. You always argue with me and it isn't right, Jake. It isn't right!"

"I'm sorry, Joanie."

"I have to have this time to myself in order to . . . do you think it's silly for me to say I must purify myself?"

"I don't think it's silly at all, my dear."

"Those people." She was still staring at us without seeing us. "In the corner. They're not really worth arguing about, are they? They deserve whatever. . . . Anything you want to do with them is all right. Get rid of them any way you like. I'm sorry I made such a fuss but. . . . It's a *sacrifice*, don't you see? I consider myself . . . maybe I'm being silly again, but I think of myself as sort of a priestess and all these distractions just tear me apart when I . . . when I want to get everything straight in my head so I can do it gently and *right* and with great *respect* for those who have to die at our hands in order that we may eventually achieve. . . ." She stopped abruptly. She pocketed the radio and turned towards the door. Over her shoulder she said in a perfectly normal voice, "Get the brats, Ruthie, while I warm up the van."

She squeezed past Frechettes' chair and strode past Ovid, at the door; a moment later the outer door to the galley opened and closed. We could hear her stride away along the dock although we couldn't see her because of the dingy curtains covering the shoreward windows.

TWENTY-FOUR

I realized belatedly that we hadn't been listening to an argument at all. It had been a ritual playlet serving some murky psychological need. The diagnosis was confirmed when I heard the girl with the headband whisper to Manny:

"Jeez, how many times do we have to watch that crazy bitch psych herself up? She always picks a fight with somebody and scares hell out of everybody with that gadget of hers. You'd think just once she'd go out and push that crazy button without all the preliminary crap, wouldn't you?"

Manny nudged her. "Shut up, here comes Fatso."

It was hard to take them seriously. They reminded me of a rather ineffectual, bickering camera club of which I'd briefly been a member in my younger photographic days. It was hard to keep clearly in mind that these particular club members dealt in firearms and high explosives and violent protest instead of cameras and films and vague aesthetic theories. There were three submachineguns and a shotgun currently visible in this rustic clubhouse, not to mention the minor artillery that might be worn out of sight and probably was. I reminded myself again that you can be killed just as dead by a mad amateur as by a sane pro.

Without looking directly at her, I was aware that Ruthie was making her way towards our end of the table, having obviously decided against inconveniencing the chairman at the other end by squeezing her bulk past him as Joan Market had done. Frechette glanced at her, impatient with her heavy, slow progress. He decided not to wait for her, and cleared his throat.

"So much for *that*," he said. "Now let's get back to the real business of this meeting. As I said earlier, the male prisoner deserves no consideration; we are justified in exterminating him like the ruthless killer he is. As for his female accomplice, let us remember that while she has not actually shed our blood with her own hands, she was instrumental in decoying. . . . What is it, Ruthie?"

I never learned what Ruthie had stopped to say. When she came to a halt nearby, looking towards Frechette and raising her hand timidly like a child in class, she had everybody's attention for a moment, and it was time to go. I threw myself forward using the back of Redband's chair to pull myself off the cot. This flipped the smaller girl backwards between me and Ovid's shotgun, while I tackled Ruthie's soft bulk and slung it straight at the muzzle of Provost's submachinegun. Very unchivalrous, no doubt, shielding myself between two women, but I was shielding Sally also, and chivalry has no place in the business. Anyway, they do keep saying they want to be treated just like men.

I was aware that the room was kind of breaking up to my right. Frechette was clawing for the automatic weapon he'd deposited on the table. Manny was rising and swinging around with his chopper. The young black in coveralls, smart fellow, was hitting the floor in anticipation of fireworks to come. A small figure flashed past behind me as I drove the big girl back against the man in the bunkroom doorway: that was Sally darting to the door and out. I felt cold air on the side of my face and heard a reassuring splash. Objective one, achieved. Objective two, personal survival, wasn't going to be that easy. . . .

The first gun to fire was the 12-gauge. Out of the corner of my eye I saw Manny crumple. . . . Manny? There was something I should remember, something I'd pushed from my mind and had to bring back, but there was no time for it now. A window broke and a submachinegun opened up. That would be Frechette turning from the confused melee inside the room to go for the clear target of the girl in the water outside. I used all the strength in my back and legs to shove the struggling, gasping, squealing mass of Ruthie and Provost, with an automatic firearm sandwiched between them, through the bunkroom doorway. Suddenly the weapon cut loose, making a single, muffled thumpthumpthump sound. Behind me, I heard the shotgun bellow once more.

"Ovid, you damned traitor!"

It was Coveralls' voice, shrill with fury. A pistol made a sharp single crack out there. Well, I'd anticipated a concealed weapon or two, hadn't I? Time was running out on me; then there was a sudden lack of resistance as Ruthie collapsed and pitched forward into the bunkroom carrying Provost with her. I tried to stay upright, but one of my legs wouldn't hold any weight for some reason. Well, I'd been hit more than once already, but I wasn't quite clear as to where or by what. I went down, landing on something hard: Provost's chopper. He'd kept a one-handed grasp of it as he tried to free himself of Ruthie's weight; but I yanked it clear, flipped it around, and hit the trigger as his shape loomed between me and the bunkroom windows. The four-shot burst cut him down. Seven gone out of what had looked like a twenty-shot clip—assuming these inefficient jerks had bothered to load a full clip.

The pistol spoke again behind me and something slugged me hard in the back. Frechette's machinegun was chattering again. You see a lot of idiot stuff on the screen, people being tossed around by bullets like leaves in a high wind. Fortunately real bullets don't pack that much punch until you get into the elephant-gun category. I swung myself around, and everything was still working—I could even get some use out of the leg. I could think and see. I had a freeze-frame picture of them: Coveralls aiming a .38-sized revolver at me, Frechette at the window aiming his squirt-gun at something outside. I swung my borrowed chopper and cleaned out that side of the room like a man painting out a couple of two-dimensional man-drawings on a wall with a well-filled brush.

When I let up on the trigger, the silence was frightening. All I could hear in the deathly stillness was the gunfire-ringing in my own ears. I pulled myself forward cautiously,

The leg would hold if I didn't ask too much of it. I knew I'd been hit in several other places, but I couldn't be bothered with that. I was looking at the room and you've never seen anything like it. Well, actually, it wasn't quite the worst I'd witnessed. Once I'd entered a crowded cellar into which somebody had tossed one grenade followed by another for luck. This wasn't quite that bad. At least they were all intact except for Manny, who'd been almost decapitated by the blast of shot from Ovid's smoothbore; and if that was supposed to make sense, somebody was going to have to explain it to me slowly and carefully. I saw that Manny wasn't the only one who'd had shotgun trouble. The girl with the gay red band in her hair had taken most of the load in the body; she lay crumpled on the floor still clinging to the chopper she'd apparently snatched from Manny's dying hand.

Ovid. It came to me then. I'd been so busy hating the little man, I'd wanted to keep hating him so badly, that I'd shoved out of my mind the fact that at Inanook he'd saved my life, or at least my sanity, from Elsie's brain-frying apparatus. Now, apparently, he'd been watching over me a second time. . . .

I was reluctant to move. I had a feeling that I would fall apart into a large number of little red squishy pieces if I tried to move. I was the last man left alive in hell, a sinner myself knee deep in the burning blood of other sinners. Well, it wasn't really knee deep but there was plenty of it, and I was in no condition to pick my way around it daintily on tiptoe. I put myself into motion very cautiously, and I didn't disintegrate but it wasn't exactly painless. I made my way slowly through the mess towards the galley door, pausing to take Manny's submachinegun from the dead girl, leaving her Provost's almost-empty weapon in return. Ovid was sitting there with the shotgun across his knees. There was blood on his shirt. The black guy in the coveralls had been pretty good with that hideout revolver. Ovid's eyes were fixed on the doorjamb ahead of him, but when I pulled the pumpgun away he looked up.

"We played hell, did we not, Mr. Helm?" he whispered.

"Hell is just the word," I said. "Who the hell are you?"

He didn't seem to hear. "Stupid," he breathed. "I should have known the Negro was armed. Ex-marine. . . . You take a great deal of nursemaiding for a man from W, Mr. Helm."

"From what?"

"W. That is what we call you in the corporation." His voice came slowly and painfully. "W for Waste. That's what you do, isn't it, waste them? We try not to come into conflict with the government at all, but sometimes the risk must be taken. It depends on the agency. But the word is out, if you touch anybody from W, you're dead. Now or five years from now. They keep a list there in Washington, and they'll waste you in their own way in their own time no matter how big you are. Fredericks in Reno. Warfel in LA—well, he got put away on a drug charge but his soldier, the one who'd hit a W agent, died with a lot of other people and it didn't do the corporation a bit of good out there on the West Coast. And in both cases W had a tall, thin trouble-shooter named Helm snooping around. . . . You don't look that good to me, Mr. Helm. I've had a very hard time keeping you alive."

"Sorry," I said. "I've been a little under the weather, I guess. Why did you shoot Kitty Davidson?"

"I had to keep the confidence of this gang of crazies by doing what they wanted until. . . . Brassaro is a fool, to get the corporation involved in something like this. When we lost his man out here and looked for another, the gentlemen of the board said to Otto Renter, give him a good boy, Otto, a boy who'll fix things for us out there and not let it get any worse, we'll handle the New York end. And Otto said to me, clean up the mess, Heinie, and don't for God's sake let that beanpole of a government man get killed or we'll have that bunch of pros on our necks. You don't have to keep him happy, Heinie, you don't have to keep him in booze and women, but keep him alive. Emilio's got us into trouble enough without stirring up W too. . . . Well, we cleaned it up, didn't we, Mr. Helm? We played hell cleaning it up. Tell Otto. . . . Tell Otto. . . ."

"Yes, Heinie," I said. "I'll tell Otto. Thanks."

He didn't hear me. I stood there a moment longer, looking down. The corporation, the syndicate, the Mafia, Cosa Nostra. Pick your own name. It will probably be no wronger than mine. It isn't my field, exactly, but as Heinie had indicated, I'd tangled with that loose-knit organization of crime a few times. Apparently I'd made enough of an impression, or Mac's agency had, to save my life today. . . .

"Ruthie." The voice was faint from outside, from shorewards. "What's holding things up, Ruthie? What was that noise? I couldn't hear inside the truck with the motor. . . . Is anything wrong, Ruthie?"

I heard somebody say, "No. Go away, damn you. I don't want to. . . . It's enough. Go away."

The voice was mine. But nobody cared about what I wanted. I wasn't here to satisfy my wants. I looked at the two guns I held. Shotgun forty yards certain, no more. Chopper maybe a little farther, fifty or sixty. Not good enough. I laid them aside and stepped over Ovid's body into the galley and got the rifle case I'd seen there earlier. It was on the counter in the galley. I hated to use, at any distance, a weapon sighted in by somebody else, even a pro like Ovid, but I had very good reason to know this gun would hit dead center at two hundred yards; after all, I'd seen one of its targets.

I slipped the weapon out of the plastic case, took the caps off the scope, and got a box of shells from a zippered compartment. I took out one cartridge, pulled back the bolt, slid the shell into the chamber, and closed the bolt on it. The safety was off. Holding the weapon gingerly, the way you do a piece that's ready to fire, I moved to the galley door.

"Hey, Ruthie, what the hell's holding you, we haven't got all day? Dammit, Ruthie, what the shit is going *on*?"

She was closer now. I opened the door. She saw me, stared at me, picked up her long skirts, and started to run back up the graveled road from the pier. I put the crosshairs in the proper place, applied easy pressure on the trigger, and let the weapon fire when it wanted to, a simple, straightaway shot of about ninety yards. Then I set the gun aside. Somebody was coming up the hatch in the galley floor. I slammed the hatch closed and fastened it down, although bending over was no fun at all. I dragged my weak leg slowly back through the slaughterhouse to the seaward door, and out on deck. I stood looking out at the river, but there was nothing but driftwood to be seen. Good luck, Sally Wong, wherever you are.

After a while I had to sit down.

TWENTY-FIVE

Since I had no idea where the barge was, to start with, or even the river, I had no way of knowing the location of the hospital to which they took me, not too far away. It didn't matter anyway. If you've seen one, you've seen them all. I'd managed to learn the only thing that really concerned me: that Sally had got through okay. It was just as well for me she'd got help moving my way fast, I was told, as I'd been pretty well bled out and wouldn't have lasted much longer.

Then they pumped a lot of corpuscles into me and dug a lot of lead out. The final tally was one 9mm submachinegun bullet, two .38-caliber pistol bullets, and two little round Number One Buckshot balls. The last two hadn't done much damage. They'd apparently been strays traveling outside the killing pattern of Ovid's shotgun that, missing a human target on the first try, had passed through one wood partition and, now lacking escape velocity, had bounced around the bunkroom a bit until, almost spent, they'd found me. Nevertheless, the general consensus seemed to be that I was a hard man to kill. I gathered that some of the more sensitive members of the hospital staff weren't convinced that this was really a good thing, under the circumstances. I suppose people dedicated to saving life will always find those who take it slightly incomprehensible.

Somewhere along the line, after I was strong enough to hold a telephone, I had a talk with Mac. He laughed when he heard what we were called in syndicate circles, but said that was really a very satisfactory attitude for them to have, and maybe in the long run it would save other agents' lives as it had saved mine. He said that, judging by the reports that had reached him, I didn't seem to take my inactive status very seriously so he wasn't going to. I got the impression he hadn't even started the necessary paperwork; he'd known I'd be back. We always come back to him in the end.

"Cut it out," I said to Ross one day. "You're talking as if they were people and I ought to feel guilty or something. A terrorist isn't people. Regardless of how wonderful his motives may be, he's something that's resigned from the human race." I grimaced. "Okay, I'm prejudiced. I feel about them exactly the way some people feel about drug peddlers."

It was the first time we'd talked at any length. Earlier, I'd been awakened from time to time to answer questions in a groggy way, but today I could see we were going to put it all together and wrap it up with gift paper and red ribbons. There was rain at the hospital windows. I remembered yearning for a tropical isle; but who wants to visit a tropical isle alone?

I said, "Anybody who wants to go out and shoot a specific politician whose policies he doesn't like, okay. That's not a terrorist in my book. I may be out there trying to stop him, but okay. He's got his target identified and he's taking all the risks involved in moving in for the kill. And if he wants to bag a few specific establishment mercenaries like you, or me, okay again. That's what we're hired for; that's the risk we run. Some of us even wear uniforms to make it easier. I'll fight like hell to prevent it, but the guy is still a human being as far as I'm concerned, even when he's trying to kill me. But these creeps are destroying exactly the human values they claim they're trying to save. They go out and do it the easy way, the coward's way, just blowing up anybody who happens to be handy, practically without risk, counting on just the concern for human life and dignity we're not supposed to have. . . . You'll notice that there's not a hell of a lot of terrorism in the real authoritarian countries. You can't scare those governments by exploding a few citizens at random. They won't hand you the keys to the Kremlin just to keep a bomb from going boom way off in Irkutsk or Petrovsk or wherever. It's only in our kind of softhearted society that this kind of blackmail works. In other words, they're trying to profit from exactly the human feelings they claim we don't have, and to hell with them."

I'd had a lot of time to think about it, lying there, and I had it all worked out, but I could see he wasn't greatly interested in my philosophical conclusions. I looked at the big, healthy-looking, brown-faced guy parked beside the bed, who hadn't even got shot once. I was way ahead of him on projectile count. He could play Mountie for a lifetime and never catch up, and it gave me a strong sense of superiority which I tried to conceal out of regard for his feelings. I guess I was still in a kind of friendly demerol haze. Otherwise I wouldn't have worried about making Mr. Michel Ross feel bad. He'd never been one of my favorite people.

"Did you ever find that bomb?" I asked.

"Yes, we found it," Ross said. "Well, the girl told us. The plump girl."

"Ruthie?" My voice still sounded weak and far away, but it was improving. "So Ruthie made it?"

I felt a little bad about having used the girl for a shield. I guess I hadn't quite dismissed all terrorists from the human race, regardless of my stern philosophic principles.

Ross nodded. "They say she'll walk all right eventually, with proper therapy. Of course she won't have much opportunity for hiking where she'll be going for a number of years. She's hardly built for it, anyway."

"Anybody else?"

"If you're worrying about your attractive Chinese partner, you asked about her when we found you, remember? Miss Wong is perfectly all right. She was suffering a bit from exposure, of course, but after one night here she was pronounced fit to go home." He hesitated. "As far as the other people on that barge were concerned, the ones who were down below got out through a hatch aft. Apparently they didn't like what they saw in the cabin. They didn't pause to sort the living from the dead. They simply ran.

We've rounded up most of them. I don't blame them for running. It wasn't pretty."

I said, "No, but just think of all the pretty things you'd have got to see if that bomb had gone off."

"I wasn't criticizing," he said mildly.

"Well, that's a refreshing change," I said. "Where did those two kookie females plant that damned firecracker, anyway?"

"At the airport," Ross said. "Timed right, it would have wiped out most of the incoming passengers from an international flight, origin New York, plus the people waiting to greet them. But of course it wasn't just a question of setting a timer, was it?"

"No," I said. "They were going to set it off on signal, they said. Brassaro was sending somebody to let them know when."

"Yes, we have a description from Ruthie. We're looking for him," Ross said. "We also have . . . somebody else. Are you up to seeing some visitors? These people have asked to be allowed to speak to you."

I shrugged. That was a mistake. After I'd caught my breath, I whispered, "Hell, send them in, whoever they are."

He went to the door and pulled it open. A man and a woman entered. I knew the man. He was Dr. Albert Caine of the Inanook Sanitarium, as well-dressed and distinguished-looking as ever, holding his pearly-gray hat in his hand to reveal the smoothly brushed, handsomely frosted, dark hair. The woman, I'd never seen before. She was tall and blonde, and quite attractive if you like ladies dressed in natty men's suits complete with zip-up-the-front pants, sharply tailored jackets, neatly buttoned vests, soft white shirts, and loosely knotted four-in-hand neckties. It's a very fashionable female costume now, I understand, but it still looks musical comedy to me, like an old movie with Marlene Dietrich singing up a storm in white tie and tails.

The woman was carrying a raincoat. There was something a bit off-key about her face. As her expression changed to register conventional sympathy for the bandaged gent in the hospital bed, I realized that not all the facial nerves and muscles were operating properly. It wasn't quite a mask, but it wasn't a real, home-grown, organic human face, either. It was the face of a handsome woman whose features had been rebuilt after a terrible accident, or a brutal beating. That placed her, of course, but it didn't seem diplomatic to say so.

"Mrs. Emilio Brassaro, Mr. Matthew Helm. And you remember Dr. Caine, of course, Helm." Ross glanced towards the woman. "Mrs. Brassaro would like to tell you about Operation Blossom."

The woman said, "I'm Blossom." A little color came into her face and she threw an odd, shy look at the man beside her. "Well, really I'm Grace, but Blossom is what . . . certain people call me under certain circumstances, if you know what I mean. Unfortunately, my husband got hold of a letter, a love letter in which. . . . Well, anyway, I'm Blossom, and it was me he wanted to kill. And Albert, too, of course. And I, we, just want to thank you for saving our lives, Mr. Helm. I should have known, when Emilio finally let me go like that, with noble resignation, that he had something terrible in mind for us both. . . . Thank the nice man, Albert, and we'll get out of here and stop tiring him."

He said obediently, "We're very grateful, Mr. Helm."

I didn't gather that the doctor's gratitude was a very high-quality emotion, but maybe he didn't have any of those to spare; his better emotions all seemed to be engaged elsewhere. They weren't people I really liked, either of them, but it was nice to see them together. You had to hand it to both of them, I reflected. At least they'd known what they wanted, each other, and even Emilio Brassaro hadn't been able to stop them in the end, although he'd come close. I watched the door shut itself behind them.

"We've really got nothing serious against Caine," Ross said. "With all the ramifications and complications of the case, it seems simpler just to let him proceed to Mexico according to plan, with the grieving widow."

"Widow?"

"Yes, Brassaro was shot down in New York two days ago. A professional hit, as you Yankees call it. Your narcotics people are disappointed. After learning how her husband had planned to murder her, Mrs. Brassaro had just supplied them with sufficient information to justify an arrest."

I grimaced. "All this just so a gangster could silence his wife, or get final revenge for being cuckolded? It seems like overkill, if you'll pardon the expression."

"I don't think you quite understand," Ross said. "The machinery was there. I believe Brassaro was beginning to think it had outlived its usefulness; he was feeling the syndicate pressure. He simply decided to employ it once more, for a private purpose, before shutting it down altogether. But it was originally set up, not for revenge, but for profit. We have reason to believe he made a good half million U.S. dollars off McNair, for instance."

"McNair?" Then I remembered that I'd read the name in a newspaper in another hospital, a long, long time ago.

"Andrew McNair. One of our Canadian politicians with controversial policies and very wealthy enemies. He was killed in the Tsawwassen ferry explosion. And in San Francisco, in the bus station that blew up, a crusading district attorney died who was embarrassing some powerful underworld figures in another city. In St. Louis I believe the airport blast removed a certain stubborn businessman who stood in the way of a multi-million-dollar international merger. . . . I could go on, but you get the general idea. I gather the price was a half million a head. Discreet human eradication, our specialty. Perfect safety guaranteed. No embarrassing murders, no suspicious accidents. Well, of course it *was* murder, but nothing that would cause any awkward questions to be asked of the victim's enemies, just the random, vicious, obvious handiwork of a bunch of known crackpot revolutionaries. Who'd think anybody would arrange for a whole airport terminal or bus to be blown up just to get rid of one man, or woman?"

I whistled softly. "I can see why the corporation decided to put a stop to the enterprise. They don't like anything that gets people too stirred up about organized crime. If the connection between Brassaro and the PPP had ever been made public. . . . How did he gain control of that protest group, anyway?"

"It was rather a coincidence, I believe," Ross said. "As we heard it, Brassaro's man Christofferson, whom we knew as Walters up here, was following a certain individual whom Brassaro wanted removed. The trail led into Canada. The quarry ducked into a railroad station, which promptly exploded, taking him with it. Very convenient for Christofferson. That was the Toronto blast in which the bomber, Daniel Market, was also killed in company with Miss Davidson's husband. Apparently Christofferson, who'd been far enough away to escape injury, saw a woman nearby acting suspiciously. It was Mrs. Market, who'd just seen, or at least heard, her husband die. Christofferson sensed that she'd had something to do with the explosion and, since the man he was after was dead, he tailed her to where her associates were waiting. We have all this from Ruthie, not a totally reliable source, but I believe it's fairly accurate."

I said, "So Brassaro moved in and took over control. It's still hard for me to believe that a bunch of dedicated idealists, even violent idealists, would allow themselves to be used like that."

Ross said, "Today's idealists make a point of being cynical idealists. It was either do it Brassaro's way or give up their crusade and go to jail; and their only explosives expert, self-styled, had just blown himself to Kingdom Come. Apparently that older man, Frechette, prided himself on being a practical chap and talked the rest into it. From then on, the PPP set off its bombs where and when Brassaro ordered, in return for supplies, arms, and protection as required. Christofferson, acting as a liaison officer of sorts, both helped them and kept them in line. Finally, as Walters, he disappeared in that plane with you; and Brassaro was forced to recruit another tough chaperone for the PPP—a chaperone who, it turned out, was actually working for people higher up in the syndicate who feared that the bloody stink of Brassaro's murderous enterprise would stick to them, too." Ross looked at me hard. "I won't ask if you've recovered from your amnesia as far as Walters' disappearance is concerned. Miss Wong let something slip that makes me think that, as a conscientious officer of the law, I don't really want to know any more about the incident than I already do."

I said, "Thanks, I can't remember a thing about Walters since you say so." I studied him for a moment. "You're not raising as much hell as I expected, *amigo*. Last time I fought my way out of a trap up here in Canada, you really laid into me for picking on those poor little helpless asylum guards and attendants. What's so different about shooting my way off a barge? Well, almost off a barge."

He was silent for a little, then he said rather stiffly, "Whatever your methods, you did prevent a terrible tragedy at the airport, Helm." When I didn't speak, he made a sharp little gesture and went on: "Damn it, man, how can I criticize your methods when mine almost got you killed? This time I'd promised you protection, remember? You and . . . and Miss Davidson."

The thought had occurred to me, but I hadn't really expected it to occur to him. Maybe there was more to the guy than I'd judged.

I said, "You lost two men trying, didn't you? At least I figured they must have been taken out, both the one you had guarding Kitty, and the one watching over me." Ross nodded minutely. I said, "Hell, you could hardly expect them to have to cope with a full-scale guerilla raid."

I didn't know why I was trying to defend him, except that he didn't seem interested in defending himself. He shook his head impatiently, dismissing my arguments. He was looking at me without seeing me.

"She looked . . . very helpless lying there in her pretty dress, didn't she, Helm? So small and helpless. And I was the one to whom she'd come for protection in the first place, when she realized she'd tackled a bigger and more dangerous job than she could handle." His eyes focused on me. "I let her die," he said bitterly. "I was angry. I thought she'd made a poor choice in you; to be frank I still do. So I took the first two men who happened to be handy and put them on the job regardless of qualifications and said to hell with her and marched away. . . ." He stopped, looking at me hard. "I'll tell you something,

Helm. Bomb or no bomb, I'm *glad* you wiped out those homicidal lunatics, you and that little St. Louis gunman. God help me, I wish I'd been there with you. When we rounded up the rest, I found myself looking for an excuse to finish the job. If one of them had raised a finger to resist, I'd have mowed down the bloody lot. What kind of a law-enforcement officer does that make me?"

I said, "A human one, I guess. Is there any other kind?" After a little, I said, "She was a sweet kid."

It sounded corny and inadequate, but I saw that he understood what I was trying to say. We were silent for a little. I realized there was no longer any question of race between us. We were just two men who'd loved the same girl, now dead. After a few seconds, he gave me an abrupt nod, and left. In the morning, Sally Wong came to see me. I called her my favorite narc, and she thought I was criticizing her occupation again—maybe I was—and said that now that we'd saved each others' lives there was really no need for us to keep fighting like that, was there?

We didn't.

MYSTERY ADVENTURES

- [ ] THE BLACK PEARLS—Kerr   23036-8   1.50
- [ ] THE DAY OF THE DOPHIN—Merle   23240-9   1.95
- [ ] FIRST BLOOD—Morrell   22976-9   1.75
- [ ] HARRY'S GAME—Seymour   23019-8   1.95
- [ ] THE MAN WHO WASN'T THERE—   23168-2   1.75
  MacLeish
- [ ] THE MATTER OF PARADISE—Meggs   22942-4   1.50
- [ ] NIGHT CHILLS—Koontz   23087-2   1.75
- [ ] THE RUNNING OF BEASTS   23061-9   1.75
  Pronzini & Malzberg
- [ ] SATURDAY GAMES—Meggs   Q2693   1.50
- [ ] THE SIXTH DIRECTORATE—Hone   q22938-6   1.75
- [ ] SKIRMISH—Egleton   Q2867   1.50
- [ ] THE SNOW TIGER—Bagley   23107-0   1.75
- [ ] SNOWBOUND—Pronzini   Q2408   1.50
- [ ] SPY COUNTERSPY—Popov   Q2435   1.50
- [ ] THE SPY LEOPARD—Forbes   23129-1   1.95
- [ ] THE TEARS OF AUTUMN—McCarry   C2649   1.95
- [ ] TESTAMENT—Morrell   23033-3   1.95
- [ ] THIS SUITCASE IS GOING TO   Q2778   1.50
  EXPLODE—Ardies
- [ ] THE TIGHTROPE MAN—Bagley   23159-3   1.75
- [ ] TIGER RAG—Reed   23173-9   1.75
- [ ] TWO-MINUTE WARNING—   23080-5   1.75
  LaFountaine
- [ ] YEAR OF THE GOLDEN APE—Forbes   Q2563   1.50
- [ ] ALWAYS LOCK YOUR BEDROOM DOOR—   13674-4   1.50
  Winsor
- [ ] CLUB CARIBE—French   13772-4   1.75
- [ ] DESERT CAPTIVE—Tokson   13722-8   1.75
- [ ] DROP INTO HELL—Cameron   13611-6   1.50
- [ ] FIRE KILL—DaCruz   13676-0   1.50
- [ ] HUNTER'S BLOOD—Cunningham   13794-5   1.75
- [ ] STRIKE FORCE 7—Mac Alister   13618-3   1.50

Buy them at your local bookstores or use this handy coupon for ordering: